W9-BUE-277

The way Leah looked at him with such hope and trust made his gut clench.

"Don't be thinking I'm some kind of hero," Roman told her. "I'm not. I'm just a guy doing his job."

One side of Leah's mouth curled. "If you say so."

"I do. Good night," he said and retreated as quickly as he could.

He had no illusions. He hadn't been able to save his mother all those years ago. He couldn't save anyone. He could find the truth, he was good at that. But that's as far as he'd go here.

When the truth was revealed, he would have to walk away from Leah. He couldn't get caught up in her just because he liked her spunk and found her attractive.

He'd be a fool to allow himself to form any kind of attachment. Because odds were she was guilty of murder.

* * *

WITHOUT A TRACE: Will a young mother's disappearance bring a bayou town together...or tear it apart?

TERRI REED

At an early age Terri Reed discovered the wonderful world of fiction and declared she would one day write a book. Now she is fulfilling that dream and enjoys writing for Steeple Hill Books. Her second book, *A Sheltering Love,* was a 2006 RITA® Award finalist and a 2005 National Reader's Choice Award finalist. Her book *Strictly Confidential,* book five of the Faith at the Crossroads continuity series, took third place for the 2007 American Christian Fiction Writers Book of the Year Award. She is an active member of both Romance Writers of America and American Christian Fiction Writers. She resides in the Pacific Northwest with her college-sweetheart husband, two wonderful children and an array of critters. When not writing, she enjoys spending time with her family and friends, gardening and playing with her dogs.

You can write to Terri at P.O. Box 19555, Portland, OR 97280, or visit her on the Web at www.loveinspiredauthors.com or leave comments on her blog at http://ladiesofsuspense.blogspot.com/.

HER LAST CHANCE

TERRI REED

Steeple
Hill®

Published by Steeple Hill Books™

If you purchased this book without a cover you should be aware
that this book is stolen property. It was reported as "unsold and
destroyed" to the publisher, and neither the author nor the
publisher has received any payment for this "stripped book."

Special thanks and acknowledgement to Terri Reed for
her contribution to the Without a Trace miniseries.

STEEPLE HILL BOOKS

Steeple
Hill®

Recycling programs
for this product may
not exist in your area.

ISBN-13: 978-0-373-44342-0

HER LAST CHANCE

Copyright © 2009 by Harlequin Books S.A.

All rights reserved. Except for use in any review, the reproduction
or utilization of this work in whole or in part in any form by any
electronic, mechanical or other means, now known or hereafter
invented, including xerography, photocopying and recording, or in
any information storage or retrieval system, is forbidden without
the written permission of the editorial office, Steeple Hill Books,
233 Broadway, New York, NY 10279 U.S.A.

This is a work of fiction. Names, characters, places and incidents are
either the product of the author's imagination or are used fictitiously, and
any resemblance to actual persons, living or dead, business establishments,
events or locales is entirely coincidental.

This edition published by arrangement with Steeple Hill Books.

® and TM are trademarks of Steeple Hill Books, used under license.
Trademarks indicated with ® are registered in the United States Patent
and Trademark Office, the Canadian Trade Marks Office and in other
countries.

www.SteepleHill.com

Printed in U.S.A.

For I know the plans that I have for you, declares
the Lord, plans for welfare and not for calamity,
to give you a future and a hope.

—*Jeremiah* 29:11

I want to say a big thank you to my cohorts in writing this series: Margaret Daley, Robin Caroll, Shirlee McCoy, Patricia Davids and Roxanne Rustand. It was fun working with you as we explored all the possibilities of the series.

To Leah and Lissa, as always, I'd be lost without you.

To Kelly and Maddie, thanks for your friendship.

PROLOGUE

Pain. So much pain.

Her head, her limbs, fingers and toes. There didn't seem to be a spot on her limp body without pain.

Water splashed onto her face from above. Cold. Freezing. Rain? No, sleet. Stinging her flesh even through her sweater and jeans. An insect buzzed in her ear. Something crawled across her ankle. She twitched. More pain.

She was outside. But where?

Opening her eyelids, she cried out as the glow from the full moon overhead seared her eyes, sending flashes of brightness crashing through her brain in agonizing waves. Squeezing her eyes tightly shut again, she waited for the tiny pinpricks of white dots to subside and the throbbing to abate.

She strained, listening. A rustling off to her left, the distant squawk of a bird, the serenade of a frog closer and the chorus of mosquitoes evidently hoping to feed on her skin. But no human noise. Where was she?

More important, *who* was she?

She searched her mind but found no sense of self, no identity, no history, no memory. She fought back the panic that threatened to overtake her. Why couldn't she remember anything?

So cold. A shiver racked her body, causing a cascade of horrific aches to wash over her system.

Survival instinct kicked in. If she didn't move soon, she'd die here. Wherever *here* was. She tried to focus, to remember.

But beyond the moment of her awakening, there was no recall, only blank spaces of nothingness. She didn't know her name, where she lived or why she was here. Fear slithered through her.

She had to move, had to get out of here. She shifted and a scream escaped, the sound deafening to her ears. She hurt so badly.

Slowly, she opened one eye, letting the sharp white lunar light seep in, allowing her vision to adjust. When at last she had both eyes open, she dared not stare at the round ball shining through the cloudy night sky. Instead, she took note of the treetops, the shadows of branches bowing to the sharp wind that kicked up and blew across her face.

Closer still, she saw that she was wedged against packed mud filled with sharp, pointed rocks. She lifted her arm and pain exploded, reverberating through her system. She had to fight it, had to get up. She had to find help.

She had to find out who she was. She hoped, prayed her memory would return. Dizzying panic rose, choking her. *Stay calm.*

Sucking in a deep breath—even her lungs hurt—she moved. The burst of frenzied pain caused another scream to burst forth. Working against gravity and her own body, she managed to crawl out of the ditch and onto flat ground.

She paused a moment to let the currents of agony recede before she took stock of her surroundings again. A wall of trees, dense and dark, on one side of her, and on the other, a road that stretched for miles.

She staggered to her feet. Her limbs heavy, weighty with numbness. Her jeans and cotton sweater were soaked through, the wet material clinging to her skin. One foot was without a shoe, and the exposed toes were bone-numbingly cold. She glanced around, but the match to the ballerina-style shoe on the other foot wasn't anywhere in sight.

She stumbled to the road, despair gripping her. No lights in either direction. Only the illumination of the winter moon showing a land of shadows. And danger. That much she knew.

Wooziness threatened, and she forced her mind to stay focused. She had to stay conscious or she'd die. She didn't want to die. Deep inside, something whispered there was a reason to live, but her mind refused to reveal anything.

She didn't know which direction to travel. Right or left. Did it even matter? With heavy steps, she walked with the moon at her back, letting the light illuminate her way.

She struggled along for what seemed like hours, as the temperature dropped. Her breath puffed out in wispy clouds. If only she could make a smoke signal with her breath, but who would she signal?

No names of friends or family came to mind. Just…blankness.

She came to a bend in the road. Hope leaped to life as a lighted structure came into view. A thick stream of smoke rose from the chimney.

Please, God in heaven, please let me find help.

She didn't question the faith in God that sprang so easily to her lips. It was just there, a part of her.

She made it to the ramshackle house and up the rickety porch steps. Rapping her knuckles against the weathered, peeling paint on the door, she didn't feel the contact of wood against her numb flesh.

There was movement inside of the house. A shuffling. Muttering.

The door opened to reveal a hunched old woman, her gnarled hands gripping a metal walker. Her cloudy gray eyes, surrounded by wrinkles and age spots, narrowed for a moment, then widened. "Land's sakes, child. Get in here before you freeze to death."

Shock rolled through her. *Had I been trying to escape from this house?* "You know me?"

The old woman waved her in. "'Course I know you. You're my grandbaby, Abigail. I've waited so long for you to finally come to your senses and come back home. You've been gone for a coon's age. When you didn't show up for Christmas two weeks ago, I about gave up hope. Now, come on in here and get warmed up."

"Where am I?"

"Why, child, you're home in St. Tammany Parish, Louisiana."

The old woman gave her a stare as if she'd lost her marbles. In a sense she had. At least her memory. She hesitated before entering.

Abigail.

The name didn't resonate anywhere in the black abyss of her memory. "Abigail," she said, trying on the name.

It would do as well as any other.

"What in the Sam Hill? You're bleeding!" the old woman exclaimed, pulling her forward by the arm. "What happened to you?"

"I don't know." She entered the warmth of the house, desperately needing shelter. "Thank you, Grand-mother," Abigail murmured, and closed out the dark.

ONE

He'd found her.

Roman Black stared at the woman pinning flowered sheets to the clothesline in the yard of a run-down single-level house. The June Louisiana afternoon sun kissed the woman's short dark hair as she bent and stretched to do her work. The red tank top covered her skin but couldn't hide the bony structure of her ribs and shoulder blades.

A skirt, hanging to her ankles, appeared to be gathered at her hip with some sort of clip that made a fabric ponytail stick out. Obviously the skirt was too big.

She turned slightly, giving Roman a better view of her face.

He glanced at the photo in his hand. Yep. Had to be the same woman. Satisfaction spread through him, making him smile. You can run, but you can't hide.

The bounty hunter got out of his late-model SUV, leaving the truck parked crosswise in the dirt drive, just in case she planned on a speedy getaway. He stalked up the drive, his heavy black boots making little noise on the packed dirt and sparse gravel. As he drew closer he heard the woman's soft melodic humming. A tune familiar, yet he couldn't place where he'd heard it before.

"Leah," he said.

The woman spun around with a gasp. Her big brown eyes widened. The fight-or-flight response warred in her frightened expression.

"Leah Farley," he repeated, watching closely to see how she'd play this.

"I…I'm sorry. There's no one here by that name. How did you…?" She looked past him down the drive. "I didn't hear you drive in."

So this is the way it was going to go down. "Look, I'm taking you in, Leah Farley."

Without hesitation she turned and fled through the swaying sheets, artfully dodging and weaving.

Roman went after her, not as artfully. After fighting back the damp bedding that clung to him, he burst through to the other side into the backyard that was nothing but a patchy lawn on the edge of a dry field.

A door to his left banged shut. The loud click of a bolt sliding home rang in his ears. He ran up the porch stairs and pounded on the door. "Open up!"

From the other side of the wooden door, he heard shuffling and frantic, whispered chatter.

He pounded his fist on the door again. "Leah Farley, open this door on the count of three or I'll bust it down."

No answer.

Roman ran a hand through his hair. Man, he hadn't counted on her being so difficult, but then again, she *was* a murderess.

One, two, three. Using all two hundred twenty

pounds of his weight, he rammed his shoulder into the door. The lock popped. The door flew wide-open.

He stumbled inside and quickly regained his balance in a ready-to-fight stance. And found himself staring down the business end of a rifle.

He held up his hands, palms out. "Whoa. Take it easy, now."

His gaze traversed the rusted and ancient-looking double-barrel to the equally ancient-looking woman holding the weapon. Though clouded with age, eyes the color of a stormy sky stared at him from a wrinkled face that the passage of time hadn't been kind to. Even her floral, shapeless housedress looked faded, as if she'd washed and worn it a million times.

Just beyond the old woman's shoulder stood Leah, bracing the rifle-toting granny as if the older woman might topple over.

Roman had two options that he could see. Talk the woman holding the gun into putting it down or take a chance that she wouldn't be quick enough to pull the trigger before he disarmed her.

Forcibly disarming an elderly woman didn't appeal. "Put the gun down and let's talk this out."

"You've got no right to come busting in here like this. Who do you think you are? If you're a police officer, I want to see your badge," the old woman demanded.

"I'm not with the police, ma'am. Name's Roman Black, and I'm here to take Leah Farley back to Loomis to face the consequences of her actions."

"We don't know any Leah Farley. This here is my grandbaby, Abigail."

Granddaughter? No way. He was certain the young woman standing before him was Leah Farley.

She might look a tad different; her long, curly hair had been shorn to a spiky 'do that made her look more like a teen than a woman in her midtwenties. She'd lost weight, which only accentuated her high cheekbones and straight nose.

She looked too much like Clint, Leah's brother, for the woman not to be Leah. He shrugged and pulled out the picture tucked away in the pocket of his T-shirt and held it up for inspection. "Ma'am, your Abigail is a dead ringer for the Leah Farley in this photo. And she looks a lot like her brother, my friend Clint."

The elderly woman glanced at the photo. Doubt entered her cloudy gaze. "You've made a mistake."

"If I have, then the authorities can straighten it out. My job is to bring this woman into custody. If she's really your granddaughter, she'll be set free. But you don't want to be charged with aiding and abetting a known fugitive, do you?"

More doubt crossed the older woman's features, and the barrel of the gun dipped toward the floor.

Pressing the issue, Roman said, "You wouldn't like prison, ma'am. It's very nasty." He stepped forward and slowly, gently, so as not to startle her into firing, wrapped his hand around the barrel.

"She's my granddaughter," the old woman insisted as she relinquished her hold.

"Then everything will be just fine." Roman checked the rifle. No shells. "An unloaded gun isn't much protection," he muttered as he stood the weapon on its butt against the doorjamb. He moved past the grandmother and secured Leah by the arm.

She winced and drew back. "Please, my name is Abigail Lang and this is my grandmother, Colleen. She needs me. You can't take me away."

"I'm sure there are social services that can help her. You are my only concern."

He pulled her toward the door.

She dug in her heels. "How come? How come you are doing this? You said you weren't a cop. So how come?"

"You can't just take her," Colleen said, her hunched shoulders shaking and her breathing coming fast as she kept pace with them while he propelled Leah forward.

"You should go take a rest, Ms. Lang," Roman suggested, worried that with so much exertion the woman would collapse and then he'd have to take her with him. "I've got a job to do. I'm sure if I'm wrong, she'll be back in no time."

"Let me at least make her comfortable," Leah cried.

"Sorry, no can do. I'm not going to risk losing you again. The authorities have been searching for you since January."

"You didn't answer me. How come?" she pressed, and made a grab for the door frame.

Blocking her access, he stated, "I'm a bounty hunter hired by Dennis Farley to find his brother, Earl Farley's, murderer. That would be you. The late Earl Farley's widow."

Shaking her head, she said, "No, I didn't kill him. I didn't kill anyone."

"Look, lady, I don't care if you're guilty or innocent.

That's for the courts to decide." He propelled her down the porch stairs even as she reached out for the railing. "Don't make me handcuff you."

She stopped struggling, but the fire of determination didn't leave her eyes. "I still don't understand why you have to do this."

"I'm repaying my client a debt owed and will get a nice bounty out of the deal, as well. It's just too bad you turned out to be my friend Clint's little sister."

"I don't know a Clint. I don't have a brother."

"How come you killed him?" he asked, curious why Clint's baby sister resorted to murder.

"I don't know what you're talking about. My name's Abigail Lang. I live here. I care for my disabled grandmother. You've made a mistake."

She actually sounded like she believed what she was saying. *Whatever.* He'd been hired to find her, not determine her mental status. He led her through the drying sheets and out to the front drive.

"Grandmother!" Abigail cried out.

The old woman was slowly working her way down the front porch stairs, gripping the hand railing. She'd left her walker at the top of the stairs. She teetered and tottered and looked as if at any moment she'd tumble head over heels down the steps.

"Oh, for crying out loud," Roman growled, and headed in Colleen's direction while still holding firmly to Leah's upper arm.

When they reached Colleen, Roman and Leah steadied the old woman and helped her down the last of the stairs.

"The walker," Leah stated with a plea in her gaze.

With a roll of his eyes, Roman momentarily released Leah to grab the walker. He set the thing in front of Colleen and then took Leah by the arm again.

"If you're fixin' on taking her, you're taking me, too," the grandmother declared, her expression determinedly stubborn. Obviously, the prospect of prison hadn't deterred her.

Great. Why not? The more the merrier. Yeah, right. Brother, could this job get any more complicated? "Okay, ladies, this is how we're going to do this. I take Grams along on one condition."

"What condition?" Leah asked, her brown eyes wary.

"You don't try to escape. If you're really who you think you are, then you'll be home before supper."

Colleen huffed. "Of course, we will. I have a roast we need to cook."

Leah stayed silent, her mysterious dark eyes holding secrets. He didn't want to know what they were. He was just the retrieval service, not the investigator. He'd left that part behind years ago. "Agreed?"

She slowly nodded.

With Leah on his right and Colleen on his left, Roman marched the two ladies very slowly and carefully toward his vehicle baking in the hot June sun.

At the SUV, he maneuvered the women around the back and to the passenger side. Opening the back door, he helped Colleen inside and buckled her up. When Leah moved to go around to the other side, he caught her hand, keenly aware of how slight she was and how easily he could crush her delicate bones. He steered her to the front passenger seat. "I want you where I can see you."

The sharp ping of metal hitting metal sent Roman's adrenal glands into hyperdrive. A bullet shattered the window in the passenger door, barely missing Leah's head. She screamed and ducked.

"Get in, get in," Roman commanded. Leah climbed into the seat. "Stay down," he ordered.

Just as Roman slammed the door shut, another bullet hit the door inches from him. One second sooner and that bullet would have been embedded in Leah.

In a crouch, he ran around the front of the SUV to the driver's side. Thankfully, he'd left his keys in the ignition, though he hadn't anticipated a gunfight or a car chase.

He started up the SUV and spun the tires as he turned the wheel and pressed the gas, shooting them forward down the drive to the two-lane highway.

Right or left? He didn't know where the shots had come from, so he could only choose a direction and pray they didn't run into an ambush. Right took them toward Loomis. The logical choice would be to take her in and collect his money.

He turned left, because obviously someone wanted Leah dead, not returned.

A dead bounty meant no money.

But a dead Leah also meant not finding out the truth for Clint, and justice wouldn't be served.

Why would someone *not* want Earl Farley and Dylan Renault's murderer brought in?

The deeply ingrained need to bring the bad guys to

justice wouldn't allow Roman to abandon this woman, especially since he wasn't sure she was the bad guy.

Roman drove at breakneck speed down the highway, heading into the swamplands of the Louisiana bayou. Tall, bald cypress trees silver-green with moss loomed, their ancient branches hanging like spidery fingers reaching out to capture the unsuspecting.

The woman beside him gripped the dash with both hands.

The old woman repeatedly gasped, "Oh, my!"

In the rearview mirror, a small red car gained on them. Roman pressed harder on the gas, pushing the SUV to the limit. The huge engine wound out with a roar. Up ahead, the road curved.

Behind them, the car closed the gap. A sports car. Go figure.

Roman cranked the wheel, tires squealing as they took the curve. For a moment the car behind them wasn't visible.

Roman's gaze snagged on a dirt road to the right. Without hesitation, he turned the vehicle down the unpaved path, which was full of potholes. The SUV bumped along, leaving a trail of dust in its wake.

Behind them the little sports car turned onto the dirt road and came to a sliding halt. Roman smiled and kept driving until he couldn't see the car anymore. He didn't have any idea where they were headed, but the road had to lead somewhere. He slowed to a more reasonable speed.

Wanting to figure out just what was going on, he asked, "How come someone wants you dead, Leah?"

"I don't know. I honestly don't know," she whispered.

Roman stepped on the brake and brought the car to a grinding halt. "Are you Leah Farley?"

Leah sank back against the door, her shoulders slumped. "I don't know. I can't remember anything before the day I woke up in a ditch and found my grandmother's house."

"You woke up in a ditch?" Roman asked, his voice rife with doubt.

"I know it sounds far-fetched, but it's true. One day last January I awoke alongside the road. My head was bleeding and I was all scraped up."

"You should have seen her," Colleen interjected. "I declare. Such a mess. Her hair was matted and her clothes torn and caked with dirt. Couldn't even remember me, her own grandmother."

"I honestly have no memories before that day." Tears slipped silently down Leah's cheeks. The heartbreaking agony on her face twisted a knot the size of the state of Louisiana in Roman's chest.

Not sure whether to believe her or not, Roman steeled himself against any softening. He couldn't let emotions sway him. The story seemed too convenient, yet she sounded sincere.

Six months ago she'd dropped her daughter off at her brother Clint's and disappeared. If what she said was true, it sounded as if she'd been taken against her will. Who took her? Why?

Plus, obviously someone wanted her dead.

Until he knew who and why, he wasn't taking her back to Loomis.

He took out his BlackBerry and activated the GPS, then scrolled through the commands until he had the information he wanted. He started up the engine.

"Where are we going?" Leah asked, her voice nervous.

"This road will take us to Tangipahoa Parish, and I know a place we can go while I try to figure out what's going on."

"You're not taking me in?"

He shifted into Drive. "No."

"But what about your bounty?"

"Justice is more important than money," he stated his own personal mantra. "Besides, I consider your brother a friend, and even though I owe your brother-in-law, Dennis, a huge debt of honor, something hinky is going on. I'm reserving the right to a grace period before collecting my cash."

"Thank you."

"Make no mistake, lady. If you are Leah Farley, and if you did kill those men, you are going to jail."

"But I didn't," she protested. "I couldn't. I mean, I don't think I could."

The frustration and fear in her eyes was real, making Roman believe that maybe she was telling him the truth. "Then we better figure out who did."

They drove in silence for a few miles before Leah asked, "You said you owe Dennis Farley a debt of honor. Did you serve in the military together?"

One side of his mouth lifted. "No. Dennis saved my life one night after I'd been shot by a bail jumper."

"You were shot? How awful," she said, sympathy reverberating in her tone.

Remembering the horror of that night brought back the strange yearning he'd felt as he'd lain there bleeding, believing he was going to die. He'd cried out to God in desperation, like some clichéd tale. God had evidently been listening. The parable of the Good Samaritan would forever have personal meaning to him.

An hour later, Roman brought the vehicle to a halt in front of a weathered, clapboard house.

"This is where we're going to figure things out?" Leah asked with disbelief.

Roman agreed the farmhouse wasn't much to look at, but it was his, left to him by his mother's parents. He and his mother had lived here before she died. "It may not be the Ritz, but let's hope no one knows about it."

With his laptop case slung over his shoulder, Roman helped Colleen out of the SUV and up the two concrete stairs to the covered entrance. Using a key on his rabbit's-foot key ring, he unlocked the door.

"Who owns this place?" Leah asked as she stepped inside.

"I do." He didn't watch to see her reaction. Her opinion of him or the house didn't matter.

As he entered, he looked at the place with a fresh perspective, that of a stranger. The years hadn't been kind to the inside. Flowered wallpaper, yellowed with age, curled along the seams and baseboards. Knotty pine floors that once had shined now were dull and dusty.

When he'd come to stay with his grandparents every summer while his mother worked, the house had been spotless and the world a wonderful place. He helped his grandfather with the chores. Back then there were animals for milking and a garden for tending, and then they'd spend hours fishing on Lake Pontchartrain.

But after his grandfather died of lung cancer and his grandmother succumbed to pneumonia, twelve-year-old Roman and his mother had moved in. And life was never the same.

Sadness filtered through his stoic reserve. There weren't many happy memories here now, only guilt, thick and oppressive, weighing on Roman like heavy bricks tied to his back.

Forcing away the unwanted emotion, Roman led the women into the living room where he settled Colleen in a leather recliner. The chair squeaked with disuse as she relaxed back against the cushions.

"I declare, I can't remember the last time I've had this much excitement." She held a hand over her heart. "I'm surprised my old ticker is still kicking, what with bullets flying and car chases."

Leah knelt beside Colleen. Taking the older woman's hand in hers, Leah said, "I'm sorry to have put you through such an ordeal. This is entirely my fault."

"Nonsense, child. I wouldn't have missed this adventure for the world." Colleen touched Leah's cheek.

Uncomfortable with the two ladies' display of affection, Roman said, "Are either of you thirsty? There's a case of bottled water in the cellar along with some other food supplies."

"In the cellar?" Leah questioned.

"It's good to have a safe place in case I need to lay

low for a while." *In case I ever find the man who destroyed my mother's life.*

He gestured to the laptop he'd carried in from the car. "I'm going to do some digging, see what I can find out about your husband's death and that of Dylan Renault."

"Who is Dylan Renault?" Leah asked, her expression puzzled.

Colleen snorted. "A no-good louse just like his great granddaddy, if you ask me. The Renaults practically run Loomis. But it's the Pershings who own most of the property downtown, which, let me tell you, fries Charla Renault's hide to no end."

"I remember there being a feud between the two families," Roman commented, picturing his days in high school when the Renault kids, Ava and Dylan, would butt heads with Max Pershing. Roman had had his own demons to battle, so he hadn't paid that much attention to the town's golden children.

Colleen nodded. "That there is. Seventy-some-odd years ago, Roland Renault the third married Mayor Scooter Pershing's daughter. I was just a little girl, but my own mama witnessed Ronald's philandering ways, which led poor Melinda to commit suicide." Colleen shook her head. "Such a tragedy. She was pregnant at the time."

"That's awful," Leah said.

"Yes, it is. The two families have been fighting over land, mayorships, friends and anything imaginable ever since," Colleen concluded.

"And the police think I had something to do with Dylan Renault's death?" Leah shook her head. "I can't even picture Dylan, let alone Earl Farley. How come the authorities believe I killed these men?"

"That's what I'm going to find out," Roman replied, pulling out his BlackBerry and punching in a number. "I have a contact on the Loomis police force. I'm going to see what he can share with me."

He could only pray the information would be helpful and not damaging to the pretty, fragile lady in his charge.

Leah watched as Roman wandered off to another part of the house, his phone to his ear. Big and brawny, with thick, dark hair and black-as-night eyes, dressed in black jeans, a black T-shirt and black boots, he reminded her of the hunter in the *Terminator* movies she'd recently seen on Colleen's old RCA television set. Leah prayed Roman turned out to be more like the Terminator in the second movie, where his sole mission was to protect.

Because obviously she needed protection.

But from whom? She clenched her fists.

She'd known the day would come when she'd be found, but she'd hoped to have her memory back first.

In the spring while shopping for some supplies in Folsom, she'd discovered the truth: she wasn't Abigail Lang, as Colleen professed, but Leah Farley. Mother of three-year-old Sarah Farley.

That hurt the worst. Why couldn't she remember her daughter, at least?

An ache deep in her soul throbbed. Ever since she'd seen the news article about her disappearance and abandonment of her child, she'd been plagued with guilt and fear. What if she really *did* do the things she'd been accused of?

She prayed every night that she hadn't.

Because if she had, her daughter deserved better.

TWO

After viewing the newspaper article back in April, Leah hadn't been able to stop herself from going to see her child. She'd done a little investigating of her own and hidden in the bushes near where her daughter played. The little golden-haired girl, so perfect, had brought tears to Leah's eyes. But no memories had surfaced, much to her disappointment.

"Dear, are you all right?"

Leah forced a smile for Colleen. "Just very confused and scared. I wish I knew why someone wanted to kill me."

Colleen took her hand and rubbed it. "God will protect you. He has already sent us Mr. Black."

"True." Though she couldn't remember her past, Leah had a deep faith in God that surpassed memory. And thinking that Roman's arrival at the Lang farm was God-ordained made her feel good, like maybe God really loved her even though she had no memory.

"I'll take a cold glass of water now," Colleen said.

"I'll be right back." Leah headed for the kitchen.

She found the door to the cellar and cautiously went

down the dark staircase. She groped along the wall until she found the light switch. The small room was indeed stocked with canned goods, bottled water and a cot with several blankets. A radio sat on a little round bedside table. Stacks and stacks of comic books lined one wall. Curious, she inspected the titles. The Maze Agency, Batman, Superman and the League of Superheroes—even Spider-Man. Quite the collection. Quite the fascination with heroes.

Did Roman have a hero complex? And what made him need a place to hide?

Did bounty hunters have to "lay low" often? From whom? The law? Or the bad guys?

She shuddered and hurriedly grabbed two bottles of water.

Though handsome in a rugged way, Roman's sheer size and demeanor scared her, yet there was something that tugged at her, making her want to trust him. Maybe it was the way he'd elected to protect her rather than turn her over. Or maybe it was the pain she sensed when they'd first walked into the house. He said he owned the place, yet she didn't get the feeling that he felt like the house was *home.*

She returned to the kitchen, closing the cellar door behind her. The freezer luckily had some ice cubes, which she took and put in a glass. He may not live here, but he maintained the property with running water and electricity. The little house obviously meant something to him, more than just a place to hide in.

She carried the ice-filled glass and one bottle of

water to the living room, where she found Colleen softly snoring.

Glad that her "grandmother" was resting, Leah set the glass and bottle on the floor beside the recliner and headed off to find Roman. They needed to talk about food, clothing and Colleen's medicines.

She found him in what traditionally would be considered the parlor, but now held nothing but a small beat-up leather love seat and a coffee table. His computer was open and running when she walked in.

He waved her over and pointed to the screen.

She sucked in a breath. There was her picture and the news article she'd seen while in the Piggly Wiggly near Folsom. Her gaze shifted to Roman. His unreadable dark eyes stared at her, piercing her all the way to her soul. She swallowed back the protestations that rose. She couldn't continue claiming ignorance of the truth. If she had any hope of reclaiming her life and her daughter, she had to take the risk and trust Roman.

What had Colleen said? *God will protect you. He has already sent us Mr. Black.*

She needed to honor the protection God provided. She had to come clean. "That's me."

He lifted his dark eyebrows. "So you admit you're Leah Farley?"

She inhaled, then released the air in a *swoosh* and her resolve stiffened. "Yes. I am Leah Farley. But you have to believe me when I say I don't remember being Leah. I only know who I really am because I read it in the newspaper and saw that picture of myself."

"What are you yammering on about?" Colleen said,

her voice rising with each word as she came tottering into the room, her walker scraping across the hardwood floor. "You're Abigail Lang. My grandbaby."

Leah reached out to take the older woman's hand. "You know I'm not. But I appreciate your trying to protect me."

Colleen's perturbed expression turned on Roman. "Now why'd you have to go and ruin everything? We were doing just fine."

Roman gave Colleen a measuring look. "Ma'am, Leah is wanted for murder back in Loomis. It was only a matter of time before someone came looking for her."

"She didn't kill those men," Colleen stated, then turned her troubled gaze to Leah. "Did you?"

Leah had no answer to that question. She hated to think she could be capable of murder, but she didn't know herself well enough to know what she was capable of.

"How come you told me she was your granddaughter?" Roman asked Colleen.

Colleen's expression turned sheepish. "At first I thought she was. I don't always think clearly. I eventually realized I'd made a mistake. She doesn't have my grandbaby's birthmark on her shoulder, but I so enjoyed having someone in the house with me I didn't have the heart to tell her the truth. I figured she'd remember her past if she was meant to on her own." Colleen shifted her attention to Leah. "When did you find out?"

"This spring. I was in town, picking up supplies, and saw the newspaper. I read about the crimes and about my…my little girl, Sarah," she said, her voice breaking. "How could I not have any memories of her?"

"You may not be my real grandbaby, but I love you like one," Colleen said, and slipped her arm around Leah's waist.

Tears spilled from Leah's lashes. "Thank you. And I thank God I found you when I needed you the most."

Roman cleared his throat, drawing the women's attention. "Do you really have a granddaughter named Abigail?"

Colleen nodded. "Yes. She lived with me from the age of six until she ran away at seventeen. I haven't heard from her since. That girl would argue with a fencepost. Not a lick of sense, bless her heart."

"I snooped around after I realized I wasn't the real Abigail. From what I was able to find out she had a wild streak a mile wide. I'm sorry she left you," Leah said.

"No reason for you to apologize. She made her choice, bless her heart. I pray every night that God is watching out for her."

"I'll add her to my prayers, as well," Leah said. Judging by the way Colleen was leaning into her, Leah decided the woman needed to sit back in the recliner. "Let's get you back to the chair before we both topple over."

Colleen allowed Leah to lead her into the other room. Once Colleen was settled in the chair with her water close at hand, Leah returned to the living room.

"It's fortunate that you found your way to Colleen's," Roman commented as she entered. "And I'm glad you decided to tell me the truth."

She dropped her gaze to his shirtfront as guilt stabbed at her. "I was afraid."

"I know," he replied softly, almost tenderly.

She lifted her eyes and met his onyx gaze. "I won't lie to you again."

He seemed to consider her words, before giving her a sharp nod. "Good. We'll need to trust each other if we hope to figure out what's going on." He gestured to the computer. "The newspaper articles about both murders coincide with the information that I was given from my contact. Earl's death at first looked like a suicide, but the forensic evidence suggests it's unlikely he could have made the shot from the angle of the trajectory." He slanted her a glance. "Speculation is you killed him, made it look like a suicide to collect the insurance money and then ran when the police started to question the suicide."

They might as well have been talking about the humid air for all the feeling his words evoked. The sensation was so surreal. Was she capable of killing a man? Especially a man she'd been married to?

Horror filled her, and fear, sharp and steady, poked her. What did she harbor inside her? Was she a person capable of killing?

Leah wrapped her arms around her middle, trying to protect herself from the dark questions. "How come I would have killed him?"

"By all accounts your marriage was rocky at best," Roman replied, his attention concentrated on the screen in front of him.

Rocky? What did that mean? Had her husband been

abusive? What about her? Was *she* the monster in the marriage? A shiver skated over her flesh. If only she could remember. But…nothing. "And what does it say about Dylan Renault?"

"The authorities are being cagey about their investigation. But apparently a shoe belonging to you was found in the swamplands near a boarded-up underground railroad tunnel where two other bodies were apparently dumped."

Leah swallowed hard, her stomach twisting. "I was missing a shoe when I woke up in the ditch."

His gaze slid to hers once again. "The shoe had blood on it."

"My blood?"

He shrugged. "Or someone else's."

Bile rose in Leah's throat and tears of anguish blurred her eyes. "How could I have done these things?" she whispered. *God, in heaven, help me.*

Roman shifted on the couch, then reached out to touch her shoulder, but he pulled back before he made contact. "None of this proves anything."

"I thought you said you don't care whether I'm guilty or not."

He blinked. "I don't. I mean…"

He looked confused and suddenly not as intimidating as he had before. His straight, dark hair feathered across his high forehead while his black eyes searched her face. With his big, wide shoulders, he looked strong and capable of protecting her. For that, she was grateful.

"Is there anyone else I might have killed?" she asked.

"Not that I know of."

"How long have you known my brother?"

"We were in the same class in high school. He saved my bacon a few times with Principal Ahrendt."

"My parents?"

He shrugged. "I don't know."

She rubbed at her temple where a throbbing had started. "Have you talked to my brother? Does he know what happened?"

"I've talked to him and, no, he doesn't know why you showed up on his doorstep with your little girl and left her there. He's worried about you. I told him I'd do what I could but that I had to bring you in."

There was someone out there worrying about her. That gave her a measure of comfort.

Roman shut the lid to the computer, the light on the side blinking, indicating sleep mode. "We should probably think about eating soon and then resting. Tomorrow, I'll go into town and see if I can look at the police reports. That might give me some clue as to why someone wants you dead."

Too emotionally wrung out to do much more than nod, Leah followed Roman into the kitchen. She leaned against the counter while he disappeared into the cellar. He returned with a bag of pasta and a can of sauce. Leah grabbed a pot and set some water to boiling, going through the motions automatically while her tormented mind tried to make sense of her life.

Nothing Roman had told her rang any bells.

She couldn't remember anything. Part of her wanted to run away and live her life without knowing, but the thought of Sarah kept her feet in place. For her daughter's sake, Leah would press through to the truth with Roman's help.

If she didn't commit these crimes, he'd make sure she was exonerated.

And if she *had* committed these crimes…?

Just thinking about the possibility made her want to hurl. Forcing her thoughts on the mundane chore of cooking, she stirred the noodles so they wouldn't stick to the pan.

When the pasta had cooked and the sauce heated, Leah went in and roused Colleen. Using her walker, Colleen shuffled behind Leah to the small mahogany dining table. As they ate, conversation was limited and stilted. Leah was glad when they all were sated and the dishes cleaned and put away in the orderly cupboard.

"There are two rooms down this hall," Roman said as he led the way and stopped before one door on the left. "This here is the master room." He pointed across the hall. "That room is a bit smaller."

"Grandmother, you take this one," Leah said, indicating the master room. She didn't really care where she slept, since she doubted sleep would come.

After digging out sheet sets from inside a brass-handled footlocker that sat at the end of the full-size bed, Roman said, "I'll be on the couch in the parlor if y'all need anything."

Leah smiled her thanks as he left them alone. She quickly dressed the bed and then helped Colleen out of her shoes before settling her back against the pillow that Leah fluffed against the worn oak headboard. She couldn't help but notice that it would have been beau-

tiful with a sanding and a varnish. The intricately de-
signed magnolia in the center caught Leah's attention.
It was a nice touch that made the rather plain headboard unique.

"Would you open the window, dear?" Colleen asked.

Leah went to the small window and slid open the
pane. Through the screen, humid air filtered in, bringing a fresh, earthy scent to chase away the musty odor
that permeated the house. Outside, the cicadas filled
the dusk with their music, a soothing lullaby. Two
massive magnolia trees filled the backyard, their white
blossoms almost fluorescent in the waning light of the
rising moon.

"That's better," Colleen said with a sigh. "I don't
have my pills."

"Don't worry. You'll be fine for the night. Roman
said something about going into town tomorrow and
I'll have him stop at the drugstore."

"Do you think we should trust him?" Colleen asked.

What choice did they have? "I think so. He seems
genuinely concerned for our safety."

"True. I reckon we're in good hands," Colleen said.
"The good Lord does provide."

"Let's pray so." Leah walked over the side of the
bed and took Colleen's frail hand in hers. "I'll just be
in the next room if you need me."

Colleen nodded, her eyes already drooping. Leah
bent to kiss the older woman's cheek before quietly
leaving the room. Once in the room that she would be
sleeping in, she sat on the edge of the full-size bed and
rubbed at her temples. She was wound tighter than an

eight-day clock, but she'd need her strength over the next few days more than ever. Because one way or another, the truth of who, and what, she was would come out.

She could only pray she wasn't as evil as the world believed.

For the second time she was placing her trust, her life, in the hands of a stranger.

Please, dear Father in Heaven, don't let me be making a fatal mistake.

A scream split the air.

Roman jerked upright and jumped off the couch. Where had it come from? The still, hot air of the house mocked him. He hadn't imagined the scream.

A low, keening wail echoed down the hall. His heart froze. Razor-sharp panic tore through him.

Leah!

Roman ran toward the room where Leah had gone to bed. Opening the door, he prepared himself to find some assailant attacking her, but instead found only Leah visible in the soft light of the moon filtering through the lace curtains. She lay on the bed, the lightweight blanket twisted around her as she tossed and moaned.

Compassion streaked through him as he approached the bed. He knew what it was like to be gripped in a nightmare, to be tormented in a way that made escape impossible. He'd had his share of nightmares. Needing to break her free of the night terror's grasp, he gently shook her. "Leah. Leah, wake up."

"No, no. Please, no," she moaned, and flailed with clenched hands.

Dodging her fists, Roman tried again, but this time gave her a firmer shake and used a sterner tone. "Leah. Wake up. You're having a bad dream."

She started awake, her big brown eyes wide as she scrambled to a sitting position. "What? What happened? How come you're in here?"

"You screamed," Roman replied, acutely aware that she'd donned one of his old T-shirts he kept in the antique dresser for a nightshirt. He swallowed back the attraction that zinged through his blood. She looked so cute and vulnerable and in need of comfort that he forced himself to take a half step back when all he wanted to do was gather her in his arms and hold her close.

She pressed her hands to her cheeks. "I did? I was trying to... Ugh, I don't remember."

Putting aside his initial reaction and thinking there might be a clue in her dream, he edged closer and sat on the side of the bed to gather her hands in his. They were ice cold. He rubbed them. "Try to remember. Where were you in the dream?"

Though the room was shadowed, he could see the frown pinching her eyebrows together. "Outside." She closed her eyes. "There was a smell. Cloying. Sweet. A bird." Her eyes flew open. "I remember a bird."

Anticipation gripped his lungs. "What kind?"

"Huge, dark. Long beak." She shook her head. "That's all I can recall."

"It's a start." Her vulnerability was getting to him. He hadn't thought it possible, but he started sweating more and it had nothing to do with the stifling heat. He released her hands and stood. "You should try to get some rest."

"Thank you."

"For what?"

"For giving me a chance to remember. For not just taking me to the police. For protecting us today."

The way she looked at him with such trust and hope made his gut clench. "Don't be thinking I'm some kind of hero. I'm not. I'm just a guy doing his job."

One side of her mouth curled up in a smile. "If you say so."

"I do. Good night," he said curtly, and retreated as quickly as he could.

He had no illusions. He hadn't been able to save his mother all those years ago. He couldn't save anyone. He could find the truth; he was good at that. But that's as far as he'd go here.

When the truth was revealed, he would wash his hands of Leah and her problems. He wasn't going to get caught up in some emotional turmoil just because he liked her spunk, and okay, found her attractive.

He'd be a fool to allow himself to form any sort of attachment. Because odds were she was guilty.

And falling for a criminal was the last thing he could allow himself to do. Not when he had devoted his life to making sure that those who deserved justice were given their due.

If only he could find the man responsible for his mother's death and exact the justice due him, Roman would be a content man.

The next morning, Roman woke to the aromatic scent of coffee. He rose from the couch and stretched to relieve the stiff kinks in his back. Plucking at the material of the T-shirt that stuck to his chest, he longed for a shower to rid himself of the sticky sweat that the humid air guaranteed he was constantly covered in.

He made his way to the kitchen where he found Leah standing at the back door, staring out at the flat, vibrant green landscape. She held a mug of steaming coffee but seemed lost in her thoughts. She'd changed back into the clothes she'd worn yesterday. He was glad she'd come clean about her identity.

Roman poured himself a full mug and took a bracing gulp. The hot liquid slid through him, jolting some life into his system. After a few minutes, he moved to stand beside Leah.

His gaze grazed over the bushes, the moss-covered trees, the sliver of Lake Pontchartrain that wound its way north, also covered in shades of green. "I once spotted a gator out there when my grandfather and I were fishing for crayfish."

"That must have made your year," she replied.

"Yeah, it did." Thinking back to that time filled him with bittersweet warmth. It wasn't long after that day that his grandfather had died. "They aren't usually easy to spot. They blend."

Seeming unperturbed by the thought of alligators in the swamps, she sipped her coffee as she glanced at him over the rim of her cup. "If we're going to be staying here, we'll need some more groceries, and Grandmother Colleen needs her meds from the house. Plus, we both will need some more clothes and toiletries."

What she said was true, but did he trust her enough

to leave her here while he ran errands? His gaze skimmed the swamps outside, treacherous ground for sure. And the road leading to the house was long and uneven. Without a car, Leah and Colleen wouldn't be able to get very far. Roman was pretty certain Leah wouldn't leave Colleen behind.

"I'll pick up what I can when I go into Loomis," he said, finishing his coffee off.

"I want to come with you," she stated, her expression determined.

"No, unless you want to be taken into custody now," he said.

"I can disguise myself as I have the other times I went into town."

He shook his head. "It's risky enough for me to go in and make sure I'm not followed. I can't be worrying about you being recognized. You make a list of what you need and I'll pick it up."

She crossed her arms over her chest. "Fine. But would you check on my...daughter, Sarah?"

"I don't think that's wise," he said. "I don't want to be responsible for something happening to her in order to get to you."

Her face paled. "You think whoever tried to kill me would go after Sarah?"

"I don't know. It is a possibility. There's already been one attempt to kidnap her."

Her eyes widened in shock. "Oh, my poor baby. Who? Why?"

"I know a man was arrested, but the FBI have been diligent about keeping the details out of the public eye." Laying a hand on her arm, he said, "But she's being well taken care of by your brother. Clint wouldn't let anything happen to her."

She blinked back tears. "Good. That's good."

He reached into a drawer beside the sink and handed Leah a sticky notepad and pencil. "That list?"

She quickly scribbled down her list, using two notes, then handed them to him. He slipped the squares of paper into his pocket.

He pulled his keys from his pants pocket and opened the back door. "You both stay inside. There's instant oatmeal in the cupboard. I'll be back soon."

"Be safe," she said as if she really meant it.

For some reason her concern warmed him to his very soul. But as he drove away he reminded himself he wasn't anybody's hero.

Especially not a beautiful brown-eyed girl accused of murder.

Leah couldn't believe that someone had tried to take her child. Little Sarah must be so traumatized. Her heart ached for all the child had suffered because of her mother. "Please, Lord, keep Sarah safe."

Colleen calling from the bedroom forced Leah into action.

She helped Colleen to the kitchen table and then made a breakfast of instant oatmeal. After they had eaten, Colleen found a stack of old magazines in the bedroom and was busily reading through them from her place in the recliner. She seemed content to relax with something to do.

Leah, however, paced the house, desperately trying to decipher her dreams while waiting for Roman to return.

When she'd first arrived at Colleen's house, she'd had nightmares but never could remember anything concrete when she awoke, only a vague sense of danger.

Now, she wore a path in the carpet of the parlor, trying to figure out the significance of the bird in her dream. She closed her eyes, conjuring up a picture of the creature. Long-beaked with a wide wingspan. Dark and forbidding. Scary. She shuddered as a wave of fear crashed through her.

Opening her eyes, her attention snagged on Roman's computer, which he'd left on the coffee table in front of the couch. The sleep mode light still blinked.

Tired of wandering aimlessly and needing to do something productive, she opened the lid and was grateful to find the desktop screen appear.

She used a search engine for the description of the bird and clicked through all the sites that came up. She mentally made a list of possible birds. Condor, vulture, pelican. Then she put each type of bird into the Web search engine until she finally found one that most closely resembled the bird in her dream. The brown pelican which happened to be the Louisiana state bird.

But all the resources stated that the bird nested on the shore, never more than twenty miles inland from the ocean. Had she been down to the seashore?

Was this memory even connected to the murders?

So many questions. But no answers. Frustration raised her blood pressure until she thought her temples would burst.

She brought up the *Loomis Gazette* and searched for anything on her daughter's kidnapping. She found a short piece about the need for more security around the Loomis Preschool after a devious man had tried to lure a toddler to the fence. Leah could only guess Sarah had been that preschooler.

Not finding anything else noteworthy about Sarah, Leah reread the articles that Roman had found the night before. The first article was about Earl Farley's death. He was found shot inside his pawnshop on the morning of December thirtieth by his wife of three years. Leah.

Her. Again, nothing she read felt like it had happened to *her.*

Leah studied the headshot photo of Earl Farley beside the article. Dark, close-cropped hair, a goatee, brown eyes and a charming smile. A handsome man to be sure, but Leah had no recollection of him at all. This was her husband? A man she'd vowed to love and honor until death.

Had she killed him? If so, why? If not, then who did? She blew out a breath, releasing some of the tension that crept into her shoulders.

She searched through the newspaper's Web site and found the article on Dylan Renault and a full-length photo of the Renault heir and CEO of the Renault Corporation. He, too, was a handsome man with a killer smile.

His hazel eyes gazed at the camera as if he were staring into the eyes of a lover. His honey-blond hair was swept back off his forehead in a casual style that belied the sharp tailor-made power suit hugging his athletic frame.

She could have been looking at any male model for all the emotion Dylan's photo provoked. Yes, he was attractive, but in a too-good-to-be-true way that didn't appeal to Leah. She much preferred the natural rugged handsomeness of Roman.

Forcing aside that errant thought, she read the details of Dylan's death. FBI agent Sam Pierce had received an anonymous lead and found Dylan's body on the grounds of the abandoned old Renault Plantation. He'd been shot in the back. At the time of the article the authorities had yet to name a suspect.

Leah scrolled through to another article. This one talked about Leah's shoe and the other bodies found in the underground railroad tunnel. There were interviews with people who apparently knew Leah. A woman named Jocelyn Pierce was quoted as saying, "This shoe only confirms that something has happened to my friend."

Leah shivered with dread at the accuracy of the woman's words and because there were more dead people associated with her name. She continued to scroll through more articles, then stopped on one that identified the deceased found in the tunnels as Amelia Pershing Gilmore and Perceval Peel.

Apparently both were locals who had been having an affair and had disappeared twenty-five years ago. The man's wife, local boardinghouse owner Vera Peel, had confessed to the murders and been arrested.

Relief oozed through Leah's veins. At least she

hadn't killed *those* two people. That was something. But why had her shoe been found there? Had she discovered the tunnel? Had Vera Peel known and tried to silence her?

Possibly the first time someone tried to kill Leah, but not this last attempt. Vera was in jail now so she wouldn't still want Leah dead. Then who would?

The headache brewing behind her eyes grew teeth, sharp and vicious. She sat back against the couch cushions and closed her eyes to rest.

The big, black bird bore down on her. Closer and closer. Its wings spread wide, blocking the light. Its sharp talons ready to rip her to shreds. A blur of red crossed her vision. Blood? She screamed and screamed and screamed.

Leah jolted awake. Her breath came in gasps and her heart beat fast in her throat. She dropped her head into her hands. What did the images mean?

Shaking off the residue of her daytime nightmare, she resumed searching the Internet for anything connected to the murders. She came across a third murder. A woman named Angelina Loring had been found dead in the swamps outside of Loomis. Though the murder occurred well after Leah had disappeared, the article stated that Ms. Loring had been seen arguing with Leah Farley only days before Earl Farley's death.

Were the murders connected?

Leah studied the snapshot of Angelina. Her flaming

red hair struck a chord. Leah concentrated on the red images in her dream. Had the red been hair?

Where was Roman? Leah glanced at the clock in the corner of the computer screen. Three hours since he'd left. How long could buying sundries and food take? But he was doing more than that. He was going to see if he could look at the police reports. Would there be some clue that would exonerate her? She hoped so.

Needing to move, Leah checked on Colleen in the next room and found the woman dozing in her chair, a magazine open on her lap. Not wanting to disturb her, Leah went back to the parlor.

On a whim she searched the Web for Leah Farley. It was strange to see her name, a name that felt foreign, come up with so many links. Most were the news articles she'd already read, but one link was to a gossip column she hadn't seen. Murderer or murdered? the headline read.

Leah's lips curled. She didn't like either scenario.

The article was more a bio on Leah, and as she read, tears gathered in her eyes because she didn't remember the parents who had died when she was in high school. Her heart ached with loss, yet there was no sense of self in the loss.

She hated the not-knowing. Suddenly she felt stifled and choked. She ran out of the house and into the swampy woods, needing the fresh air. Space.

"Oh, please, Lord, help me to remember," she cried aloud, and then sank to her knees beneath a large crape myrtle, sobs racking her body.

A noise behind her raised the hairs at her nape. Had

the person who tried to kill her found her? Would she die here and now without knowing the truth?

Run!

Fear, sharp and demanding, speared through her, staking her feet to the ground.

Move!

Before she could conquer the knife-edged terror enough to make her limbs cooperate, strong arms wrapped around her. She struggled, twisting and turning.

She wasn't ready to die.

THREE

"Shhh," Roman soothed, as he tried to calm his own racing heart. "It's me."

For a moment Leah froze, then sagged against his chest, her body melting so that it seemed as if his arms were the only thing keeping her upright.

He liked the feel of her within his embrace, liked the way their heartbeats melded together. For a second he gave in to the need to just hold her, but doing so reminded him that getting emotionally attached would only jeopardize his judgment. He needed to keep a clear head and keep his heart from going soft. Guilty or innocent, she was just a job.

He set her from him and turned her to face him. "I told you not to leave the house. You scared the daylights out of me. Are you hurt?"

She shook her head.

With the pad of his thumb he wiped away her tears. "Then why are you cryin'?"

"I just couldn't be inside anymore. I don't know how much more of this I can take," she whispered.

The turmoil in her beautiful brown eyes attested to

that. He couldn't imagine not having any memory, yet in some ways, for him it would be a blessing not to have to remember the horrors of the past. "You're not going it alone. No matter what happens, what we find out, the truth is better than living a lie."

"I hope that proves to be true," she replied.

He led Leah through the trees and across the yard back to the house. "I bought you a change of clothes and the other items you requested. The pharmacy wouldn't turn over Colleen's meds, so I had to go back to the house. I just threw all the bottles in a bag and brought them. Colleen is changing now. Does she need your help?"

Sniffling, Leah nodded. "Thank you for getting everything. I'll go see to her."

Roman watched her walk away, the skirt she'd been wearing since yesterday now caked with dirt from where she'd been sitting on the ground when he found her.

Man, he'd about come unglued when he'd walked in and discovered she was missing. His first thought was she'd reneged on her promise not to run away, but then a more horrible thought had chomped through him. What if the would-be assassin had found the house and taken her?

His heart had jammed in his throat when he'd seen her sitting on the ground sobbing. Now, he had to get a grip. She was safe and he had a mystery to solve.

But first he had to feed his guests. He made sandwiches and put out a tray of prepared fruit he'd bought from the store.

Going into the parlor to wait on the ladies, he noticed his laptop was open. Leah had obviously been using his computer. Good thing all of his files were password protected. Judging by the article on the screen, she was doing a little digging herself.

Interesting.

None of the other articles he'd read mentioned Leah had been a secretary at city hall right before she'd disappeared. Roman knew she'd worked at Renault Corporation before she married Farley and that the police considered that enough of a connection to name her a suspect in Renault's death.

"Did you find out anything when you were in town?" Leah asked, joining him in the parlor. She'd rid herself of the skirt and tank. The black jeans and dark red, scoop-neck T-shirt he'd bought for her fit her well. He thought he had not looked too closely at her, but apparently he had. That was a sobering realization.

The red of the shirt deepened the contours of her cheeks and emphasized her pretty brown eyes. He could look at her all day long.

He shook his head to give her a negative response, as well as to clear his vision. "Not much. I didn't want to draw attention by asking too many questions. The FBI is still looking for you and the sheriff has a bad case of wanting to nail you not only on Farley and Renault's murders, but also for the murder of a woman named Angelina Loring."

"I read that she and I argued on the town green a few days before I disappeared."

"Do you remember about what?"

She shook her head. "No. Nothing. Though while you were gone, that same image came to me."

"The bird?"

"Yes. Only this time there was a streak of red. Brighter than this shirt. I think maybe it was hair. Someone with red hair?"

He sat forward. "Did you see the person's face?"

"No. Just the hair. But it wouldn't matter because I wouldn't recognize them even if I knew them."

Seeing the frustration in the tight lines around her mouth, he changed the subject. "Did you read here where it says you work for city hall?"

"I didn't." Her eyebrows drew together as she peered at the text on the screen. "It says I worked for the mayor."

She sat back, her expression arrested with thought. "Do you suppose I saw or heard something that I wasn't supposed to? Could that be why I left my daughter with my brother? To keep her safe?"

The desperate and earnest expression on her sweet face did something to him. She so wanted to believe there was a logical reason why she had abandoned her child. He'd reserve caring until he knew the truth. "That is definitely a possibility. One I'm sure the feds have thought of but it's worth our checking out. And I'd like to know why you and this Angelina woman were arguing. My gut tells me her death is connected somehow to the other two."

Colleen shuffled into the room with her walker. "My bread basket needs a fillin'," she groused.

Leah jumped up to take the older woman's arm.

Roman rose, liking how solicitous Leah was with

the elderly lady even though the woman wasn't actually related. "I've made sandwiches."

"Thank you, young man," Colleen said, allowing Leah to lead her into the kitchen. Leah flashed Roman a grateful smile as he stepped closer to follow them.

For the second time they sat to share a meal together like a family. An uncomfortable disquiet stole over Roman. Last night, he'd been too preoccupied with the situation to take note of how nice it felt to be sitting with the ladies. Now, he realized how much he missed being a part of a family.

Colleen said grace before they started eating. After a few moments, she peered at Roman over her half-eaten ham-and-Swiss sandwich. "Don't you have someone wondering where you are?"

"No, ma'am," he replied, wondering how she'd picked up on his thoughts.

"A good-lookin' boy like you must have a girl. Or two."

Roman choked on a chip.

Leah patted him on the back. "Grandmother, that's not very polite."

"I'm old. I don't believe in wasting my breath with pleasantries," Colleen countered. Her gray eyes narrowed on Roman. "So. Do you?"

Somewhere between wanting to ignore the woman's prying and the need to bust a gut with a laugh, Roman shook his head. "No, ma'am. I'm too busy with my job."

"Humph. Men and their jobs."

"Grandmother," Leah said, her voice holding a note of reprimand.

"My dearly departed husband, Ed, always put family first. A man should put family first. Don't you think?"

"Yes, ma'am, I do." An unexpected dart of sadness shot right to his heart. He could barely remember his father. But Roman was sure he'd have been a man who put his family first. Though he'd been six when his father died in a sugar-mill accident, Roman could still picture his father's big, burly shoulders and easy grin. His parents had been so happy even though they hadn't had much.

Even after his father's death, his mother had tried to give Roman a good life. Until one fateful night…

Colleen arched a graying eyebrow. "And just how come you're helping us, young man?"

He darted a look into Leah's eyes, remembering her after her nightmare. So scared and vulnerable. He decided to give an honest answer. "I want to see justice done, ma'am. Seeking the truth is the only way to ensure wrongs are paid for and the innocent aren't unjustly condemned."

Clearly impressed, Colleen nodded sagely. "I like you."

Oddly pleased by her pronouncement, Roman said, "Thank you, ma'am."

"Now that I've had my fill, I'd like to go back to reading my magazines. I don't know half these young stars anymore, but it sure does make for juicy reading."

Leah helped Colleen back to the living room while Roman cleared away their plates. A few minutes later, he met Leah back in the parlor.

He grabbed a paper bag off the counter and pulled out a notepad, pens and a map of Loomis. Spreading the map out, he said, "I thought we'd see where all of these events took place and then after dark tonight we'd go see if we can jog your memory."

"Good idea," she said, and picked up the pad. "I'll start a list of what we know so far."

"Great thinking." He watched her for a moment as she wrote, her eyebrows drawn together in concentration.

He really hoped she wasn't guilty because he really liked her. Liked how determined she was to know the truth, liked how she cared for those around her. If she wasn't guilty, he really wanted to reunite her with her daughter.

He could only imagine how confused and lost her child must feel. His mother hadn't physically gone away when he was a boy, but she had checked out emotionally and mentally long before she died.

Clenching his jaw against the tidal wave of fury that always rode his back whenever he thought of that night, Roman took out his BlackBerry and sent his normal weekly text to one of his buddies, Karl, still on the Baton Rouge police force. As always, Roman asked to have the latent prints of the man who was responsible for his mother's death run through AFIS, the Automated Fingerprint Identification System.

One day, the system would come up with a name. And when that happened Roman intended to make the man pay. Because, as he'd explained to Leah, justice was the only thing he lived for.

Refocusing on the current situation, he turned his attention to the job at hand. He picked up a marker and circled the area where Earl Farley was murdered.

"I want to check out the pawnshop and your apartment," he stated. "The police have already combed through both premises and there probably won't be any clues left behind, but taking you there might trigger some flashbacks."

"How will we get in?" she asked, looking up from the list on the notepad.

He shrugged. "I'll pick the lock."

"Did they teach you that in bounty-hunter school?"

He grinned. "Naw, I learned that when I was still a kid."

She grinned back. "Sounds like you were wild. Did you grow up around here?"

He met her curious gaze. "Yes. I was in your brother's class in high school."

"That's right, you said you were friends with my brother." She made a face. "I can't remember his name."

"Clint. Clint Herald."

"And my name was Leah Herald and I grew up in Loomis. I have one brother named Clint, and I read that my parents died when I was a teen." She tapped the pen against the pad. "I wonder if I went to college. Is that where I met Earl?"

"Could be."

"How come we don't call Clint and ask him?"

"I'd rather not let anyone know I've found you yet. None of these articles go very deep into your background. But if you went to college, that is something we can check from here." He dragged the computer closer. "Let's see. What colleges are close that you might have attended?"

She watched his blunt, strong fingers traipse over the keyboard with speed that could only be acquired from frequent use.

"Loomis College," he said. "I'll hack into their system and see if you were ever a student there."

"Another trick you learned when you were young?" she quipped, marveling at the way he made the computer jump at his commands.

"No, this I learned from a computer expert on the Baton Rouge police force."

"You were a police officer?" Somehow if he had been it wouldn't have surprised her. He had an air of authority that screamed law enforcement.

"Yep. For a whopping ten years. Didn't like all the red tape tying my hands. Left the force to start my own business."

Hoping to learn more about this man who'd come charging into her life, she asked, "Where are you based?"

"I have an office in Baton Rouge."

"Are your parents still in Loomis?"

He kept his gaze on the screen, but his shoulders visibly tensed. Leaving her question unanswered, he said, "It says here you completed two years of general education."

Forcing back the curiosity that begged to pry into his personal life, she said, "Which means I didn't graduate."

He clicked off the Web page. "No, but one of the articles mentioned that you worked at Renault Corporation. I'll check their human resources files and see what I can find."

Leaning back against the cushions, she closed her

eyes. She prayed he'd find some useful information that would drive them closer to finding the truth.

But she couldn't stop the anxious little flutter in her gut, because the truth could either set her free or send her to prison.

Roman easily hacked into the Renault Corporation's employee files and found Leah's work record. Her bosses had very complimentary words about her. She appeared to be a hard worker, caring, efficient and loyal. She'd moved up the ranks of the secretarial pool to the administrative offices within a relatively short time. Before she'd given notice, she'd been assigned to work on a project with Dylan Renault as his administrative assistant.

So there was a personal connection. A fact to be considered, but not proof of any wrongdoing.

According to her records she was unmarried at the time she'd left Renault Corp.

Was she married by the time she began working for the mayor's office? Where had she met Farley?

Hacking into the city of Loomis's employee records proved a tad more difficult. Obviously someone had integrated some sophisticated protection software into their computer system. But it was nothing that Roman hadn't seen or managed to circumvent in the past.

He'd just found Leah's file when she moaned. His gaze whipped to her. She was asleep, but from the twisted expression on her lovely face and the way she twitched, he assumed she was in the throes of a nightmare.

The need to relieve her of her bad dream and the need to have her remember more warred within him.

"No, no, please," she whimpered.

Roman couldn't take seeing her distraught any longer. He touched her shoulder. She flinched as if he'd hit her. He frowned, hating the thought that she'd ever been abused.

"Leah, wake up, honey," he said, keeping his voice gentle. Remembering how difficult it had been to bring her out of her dream state last night, he gathered her in his arms and rocked her. "Shhh. It's okay, you're safe. No one's going to hurt you."

She whimpered again and snuggled deeper into his embrace. He swallowed hard. Maybe holding her had been a mistake; he didn't know if he'd ever want to let her go. It had been too long since he'd felt any kind of human connection.

She sighed and he could feel awareness come over her. At first she tensed, then softened. Her head lifted and her eyes searched his face. The terror in her eyes receded and trust filled her gaze and warmed his soul.

"You were having another nightmare," he stated. He knew he really should have let her go, but he held on, unwilling to break the physical connection yet.

"It was awful, Roman. Earl, my husband, was so angry. The images were all garbled, but there was so much rage."

"You're remembering?" His chest squeezed. When her memory returned, who would she be? "Can you remember any words he said? Where you were?"

She shook her head and eased away from him,

breaking the connection between them and leaving a cold void despite the sizzling summer air.

"No." Disappointment laced the word.

It wasn't just the truth they were after, but also getting her life back.

She gestured toward the computer. "Did you find out anything?"

"You were an exemplary employee at Renault Corporation. You worked your way up to administrative assistant for Dylan Renault."

She gasped softly. "So I knew him well."

"Apparently. You weren't married when you worked there, and I was just starting to look at your employee file at city hall when you started having your nightmare."

"Well, we're getting a better time line on my life than we had before," she said in a wry tone.

Yes, one step closer to figuring her out and moving on. Roman moved his hands back to the keyboard.

A frail scream from the other room jolted through the parlor. In a flash, Roman was up and racing to find Colleen, Leah on his heels.

As they skidded into the room, Colleen pointed at the window. "There was a man. There was a man!" she cried.

"Stay here," Roman ordered, and turned to leave, intent on finding the prowler, when an explosion rocked the house.

Leah and Colleen screamed.

Blood pounded in Roman's head. Where had the explosion come from?

The acrid smell of smoke billowed in. The bedrooms were on fire. "Hurry," he urged as he scooped Colleen from the recliner.

Holding Colleen like a child, he carried her toward the back door with Leah right behind him. As he entered the kitchen, he came to an abrupt halt. If they went out that door, they'd be picked off like ducks in a shooting gallery.

"What's wrong? How come you're stopping?" Leah asked. "We have to get out of here."

"Not this way." He led her back to the parlor and halted near the window. Setting Colleen on her feet, he said, "Turn away."

Using his foot, he smashed through the window, glass spraying both inside and out. He continued to kick at the sharp, jagged pieces sticking to the frame until none remained. He climbed out and whipped around, ready to take on any attackers. The area was clear.

"Come, Colleen." He encouraged the older woman to climb out.

Colleen hiked her legs over the window ledge, then fell out into Roman's arms more than climbed. He set her feet on the ground. She hung on to his shirt for support.

Panic swirled in Roman's head when Leah didn't immediately follow Colleen. He was about to climb back inside when she appeared at the ledge, carrying the laptop. She handed the computer to him and then deftly made it out through the window.

"Good thinking," he said, appreciating her resourcefulness. "This way," Roman instructed as he once again swooped Colleen up into his arms and ran as fast as his burden would allow toward the shelter of the ancient cypress trees.

Behind them the roar of red-gold flames engulfed the house, lighting up the night sky and destroying all that was left of his family.

As Roman led the women deeper into the murky swamp, one question pounded into his brain:

How on earth were they going to survive?

FOUR

The blaze lit the night sky and threatened exposure. Using the dense grove of cypress and sycamores for cover, the trio forged a trail deep into the bayou. The ground beneath Roman's feet turned mushy with the still waters of the swamp. Colleen shivered in his arms. He could hear Leah's labored breath beside him. He had to get them to safety.

Because the one who was after Leah had just tried to kill them all. And no doubt wouldn't stop until they were all dead.

They'd burned down Roman's house. His safe place. The only place that held any memories of his family. Sorrow tried to seep in, but the anger seething in his veins wouldn't relent. How had they been found?

He'd been careful to be sure he hadn't been followed from town. Which meant someone had discovered his family home the good old-fashioned way, by researching Roman's background.

Thankfully, he'd had his business partner, Mort Jenkins, secure lodgings in Loomis while Mort did some legwork talking to folks, following up on the leads Dennis and Clint had supplied. In fact, Roman had been following a clue when he'd found Leah. Clint had taken a drive north and had thought he caught sight of her one day. Roman had driven the same route and stopped at the local mini-mart and charmed information from the cashier. Apparently, Ms. Lang had a guest staying with her. The checker had given directions to Colleen's house. Roman had hit pay dirt.

Now his prize was in danger. He had to get the ladies to safety.

"There's a pirogue up ahead," Roman stated, indicating with his chin the direction of the small rowboat. "We'll go downstream."

Leah glanced over her shoulder into the darkness behind them. "Do you think they'll follow us?"

"Probably, but we have other things to worry about, as well." Roman couldn't keep the grim edge from his voice. He kept his gaze sharp for any sign of the gators that lived in the water.

The sounds of bushes being thrashed broke the stillness of the bayou. Their pursuers were right behind them.

"I see the boat," Leah cried, and rushed forward, the swamp mud rising to her knees.

"Hurry." Roman carried Colleen to the small wooden boat and set her down on the bench that ran crosswise. While he steadied the small craft for Leah, he kept his gaze trained on the trees they'd just waded through. Any moment he expected to see men racing to finish them off.

Once Leah was settled next to Colleen, Roman pushed the boat from the shore and jumped in. The small vessel rocked unsteadily. Not waiting for the craft to balance on the water, Roman took up the oars and began to row them farther downstream as fast as his arms could go.

Several hundred yards later when he felt a bit safer, he took out his handheld phone. The words *No service* were highlighted across the screen. Frustration thudded at his temples as he picked the oars back up and continued to row away from their attackers.

"What now?" Leah asked, her soft voice echoing through the stillness of the bayou.

"We'll keep going until I can get a signal," he replied, his arms moving the paddles in a steady rhythm. He was careful not to let the oars drop into the water. He didn't want a splash to alert any would-be predators, human or otherwise, to their presence.

"Do you want me to keep checking your phone?" Leah whispered, her hand extended.

He handed over his BlackBerry. Leah moved the rolling ball that acted as a mouse on the tiny screen and activated the light, which illuminated her face in an eerie bluish glow, making her appear ethereal. "Still no signal."

Roman kept rowing, his biceps beginning to feel the strain.

A soft splash sounded from somewhere off to their right. The moon's glow showed the ripples along the surface of the murky waters.

Colleen started and pointed an arthritic finger next to the boat. "There's something in the water."

Colleen's frantic whisper stirred the fine hairs on the back of Roman's neck. He kept rowing, praying whatever she'd seen would not take an interest. "Stay calm. As long as we don't bother nature, nature shouldn't bother us," he said, hoping his words would hold true.

Leah wrapped her arms around Colleen. "How much longer?"

Wishing he had the answer, Roman increased his effort. Every protective instinct urged him to move faster. "Try the phone again," Roman instructed.

"Got a signal," she said. "Who will you call?"

From the troubled look on her pretty face, he figured she thought he intended to call the police. Life certainly would be simpler letting the authorities have Leah, letting them sort out the mystery surrounding her disappearance and the attempts on her life. But the police would see Leah only as a suspect, not an intended victim. No justice in that. No justice at all.

"I'm calling my business partner, Mort. He should be in Loomis by now and have rented a place to stay," he said to reassure her.

Until Roman discovered who was after Leah and why, it was up to him to keep her safe and out of sight. He wouldn't be able to live with himself otherwise.

And he prayed he was making the right decision.

The soft pings of the phone dialing seemed like a loud gong in the hushed bayou. Leah's gaze drifted to the dark waters and the trees beyond the shoreline where danger lurked, watching, waiting for an opportunity. She shivered.

"Mort, Roman here. Call me asap. I need your

help," Roman said into the phone. A bead of sweat rolled down the side of his ruggedly handsome face.

That he asked for help spoke volumes of the danger they were in. Leah didn't figure Roman was a man who sought help from others often, unless the need was great. Obviously their circumstances qualified.

Fear tapped at her. How long would they have to wait here in the swamp? Would they be found before help arrived?

Roman clipped his phone onto his belt, took up the oars again and smoothly rowed, his strong arms bunching with effort. She sent up a silent prayer that he possessed enough strength to protect them.

The boat glided along for what seemed an eternity. Colleen's head lulled until she finally rested heavily on Leah's shoulder and her quiet breathing indicated she'd fallen asleep. Leah felt the need to rest, too, but she couldn't allow herself. What if she had another nightmare? Not a good idea while sitting in a small boat in the middle of dangerous waters.

"I'm sorry about your house," she said to Roman. Guilt that he'd lost his safe place gnawed at her like the mosquitoes constantly landing on her bare arms.

"Yeah, me, too," he replied, his voice full of regret and anger. "I should have known better than to take you there."

The self-recrimination in his tone made her frown. "How could you have known? It not like you're clairvoyant or anything, are you?"

He gave a short laugh. "No. But I should have thought it through better. Whoever is after you has resources at their disposal. They knew I was looking for you. They followed the rabbit trail by digging into my background and it led them here. To you."

She hated hearing his self-blame. "You were operating under the impression that I'd murdered my husband and run away. You had no way of knowing there was someone else at work here. And you took us to the only place you could at the time. I don't blame you for this. I blame myself. I should have come forward when I first read the news articles."

He met her gaze and held it, the intensity bright in his eyes despite the faint light of the moon bouncing off the water. "You were afraid," he stated.

"Yes, I was." *I still am.* But she had to get over the fear and face the truth when she found it. For her daughter's sake.

A sharp, jarring noise exploded from the Black-Berry phone clipped to Roman's belt. Birds screeched out of their nests in the trees. Leah's breath halted. A splash from off to the right echoed across the water.

"Sorry. Can't believe I didn't put it on vibrate." Roman hastily lifted the oars from the water to answer the phone.

Colleen started awake. "What's that?"

"The phone," Leah said, soothing the older woman's nerves.

"Mort," Roman spoke in hushed tones. "I need you to come get us."

He listened for a moment. "That's good. Let me see where we are. Hold on a sec while I bring up the GPS."

He pushed some buttons on the small keypad and stared at the screen before clicking back on with Mort.

"We're about two miles from a service road." He gave Mort the coordinates. "Be careful that you're not followed. Someone just tried to burn us alive in my family's home," Roman warned before hanging up. "Not long now," he said, and resumed rowing.

Leah rubbed her itching arms as Roman once again got the boat moving toward their goal. If only her memory would glide as effortlessly toward remembering.

Beside her, Colleen shivered. The night air grew cooler.

To the left, Leah could just make out a structure on the riverbank and what looked like a road leading away from the water. She pointed to it and Roman nodded as he maneuvered the oars to take the boat to the shore.

Once there, he jumped out and pulled the boat farther aground before helping Colleen out of the boat and carrying her to the rickety lean-to. He deposited her on a makeshift bench created from a two-by-four supported by two sawhorses.

Leah moved to the front of the boat and was climbing out when Roman came back to help her. His firm and comforting grip on her elbow steadied her as she stepped from the boat onto the soft shore. Her sandals sank in the marshy mud and made walking forward difficult.

She gasped when Roman swung her into his arms and lifted her from the ground. Reflexively, she hung on to his neck as he carried her to the shelter. So close to his skin, she breathed in his masculine scent and it filled her senses, making her want to snuggle close and forget the dangers waiting to pounce.

He set her on the ground and she reluctantly withdrew her arms from around him, feeling bereft of his warmth. Needing a diversion from the handsome man pacing before her, she tried to force her memory to come back. She focused on the images from her nightmares, but nothing new surfaced. When the frustration became unbearable, she abandoned that futile endeavor and instead watched Roman.

She never would have dreamed when she'd first seen him that she'd put her life into his hands. Why was he willing to protect her when he'd been so bent on gaining his bounty money?

She approached him where he stood guard, watching the water and the road. By the light of the moon, she could make out the hard line of his jaw and the watchfulness of his dark eyes.

Keeping her voice just above a whisper, not wanting to disturb the stillness of the bayou, she asked, "When I asked you the other day why you weren't turning me in, you said justice was more important than money. What does that mean? I don't think many people would turn down money for justice."

His voice maintained the same quality as hers. "More people should stand up for those who've been knocked down and knocked around. Too few have felt the bite of injustice. And many who have didn't deserve it."

Did that mean he'd been knocked around? A spasm of sympathy rushed through her. "Do you speak from experience?"

When he didn't immediately answer, she realized

he had experienced injustice—or someone close to him, anyway—and he didn't want to share the details with her. Why should he? Even though he professed to want justice, he still had doubts of her innocence. She couldn't say she blamed him. She couldn't be sure she wasn't guilty until her memory returned.

"I'm sorry, I have no right ask you that," she said, and folded her arms over her chest.

She sensed rather than saw his shrug. "It's okay."

The sound of tires squishing on the muddy service road claimed their attention. Leah steeled herself for meeting his business partner as headlights slashed through the darkness and blinded her. Would this Mort person be as concerned with justice, or would he just as soon turn her in and collect a bounty? Using a hand to shield her eyes, she instinctively moved behind Roman.

The brightness dimmed to the small orange parking lights of a big extended cab truck. The door on the driver's side opened and a man climbed out. "Hey, boss," Mort said as he ambled closer. His tall, thin frame was outlined in an amber glow.

Roman met him with a handshake. "Did you find a place?"

"Sure did. On the far side of town near the old pier," Mort replied, his gaze landing on Leah.

She ducked her chin. His lean face and wide-set eyes showed his curiosity.

"Let's get the ladies in the truck and get out of here," Roman said, and walked away to gather Colleen into his arms.

Exposed, Leah wrapped her arms around her middle.

"So you're the mystery woman," Mort said, and stuck out a hand. "Mort Jenkins, at your service."

Swallowing back the wariness that made her want to refuse his offered hand, Leah placed her hand in his anyway. Roman trusted this man, and she doubted Roman's trust was easily won. Mort's handshake was firm and brief.

"Let's get you in the truck. Roman made it sound like y'all were being chased," Mort said as he escorted Leah to the truck.

"Yes, we were—are. They blew up Roman's house." Her throat constricted with sorrow at the loss of Roman's home.

"Whew, these boys mean business then," Mort replied as he opened the door for the back of the cab.

She climbed in and then helped to get Colleen settled on the seat beside her.

Roman touched her hand briefly. "It's going to be okay."

That he was trying to reassure her was sweet. She gave him a wan smile. If only she could believe that everything would be okay.

But she didn't know what to believe. Was she capable of murder? She prayed not. And someone was out to kill her. Why? What secrets were locked in her brain?

Mort drove them around the outskirts of Loomis, past sleeping neighborhoods, to an old Victorian house. Even in the dim light of the high moon, Leah noted the house was in need of repair. The porch sagged and there were roof tiles missing. Mort parked the truck around the back, close to the door.

"Best if no one sees you ladies enter," Mort explained. "We wouldn't want whoever's after you to realize you're here."

Roman came around for Colleen and helped her inside.

Feeling conspicuous, even though the hour was so late, Leah quickly left the safety of the truck for the house. What if a neighbor was peering out a window, watching them?

She entered the back door that led to a kitchen with stained, white linoleum flooring and out-of-date appliances. The pea-green color of the walls did nothing to cheer up the room. The air inside smelled slightly of mothballs and disinfectant.

"This place could sure use some sprucing up," Colleen muttered as Roman carried her inside. She tapped his shoulder. "Set me down, boy."

"Yes, ma'am," he grinned, and complied.

Mort closed the door behind him. "This here place used to be a boardinghouse run by Vera Peel. Though her husband and his mistress were murdered decades ago, she was just recently arrested for the crime."

"There was a murder in this house?" Colleen shuddered. "I don't think I can sleep where someone's been murdered."

Mort held up his hand. "Now, I didn't say someone was murdered here. Seems Mrs. Peel did her husband and his girlfriend in at some underground railroad tunnel used to smuggle out slaves back in the day." He turned his hazel eyes on Leah. "From what I've gathered, the police were actually looking for *you* in the tunnels, Mrs. Farley, when they stumbled on the skeletal remains of the two dead bodies."

The thought that she might have been in that tunnel with the skeletons creeped her out.

"Do the authorities know who the blood on the shoe belongs to yet?" Roman asked.

Mort shrugged his thin shoulders. "The gossipmongers don't know it but there's plenty of speculation that it's Dylan Renault's."

Leah cringed and her stomach sank. Maybe she had killed Dylan. But why?

"Tomorrow I'll see what I can find out," Roman said. "For now, I suggest we clean up and get some rest."

Leah hated to point out the obvious. "We have no clothes or anything to use to get clean."

"Not a problem," Mort said. "This place came furnished and with clothes in several of the closets when I rented it from Mrs. Peel's daughter. She said the stuff was left by boarders over the years. I'm sure y'all will find something useful."

Suppressing a shiver of revulsion over wearing other people's clothes, Leah found something suitable to wear for the night for Colleen and herself. Thankfully, the garments smelled clean if a little musty.

She decided in the morning she'd wash the rest of the outfits they would borrow. After cleansing showers, Leah settled Colleen into a strange bed.

Yawning, Leah made her way to her own bed and

fell back against the down pillow, wondering if she'd ever know a good night's sleep again.

A twig snapped. The hairs on the back of her neck quivered. Danger! The silent alert boomed inside her head as pain exploded. The ground rushed up to meet her. Sharp talons reached for her. She fought to get away from the beast that gripped her. More pain as something dark smothered her. She glimpsed the big black bird, its beak hung open as if letting out a mocking laugh that chilled her to the bone.

Leah jolted awake. She scrambled to a sitting position. Her frantic gaze took stock of her surroundings. No dark bird loomed. She was safe in the bedroom of the upstairs apartment located in the old Peel boardinghouse. She took deep fortifying breaths as she tried to make sense of the dream.

Closing her eyes, she realized she had glimpsed something else.

Something she hoped would be a clue.

The next morning, Roman and Mort joined the ladies for coffee and beignets, compliments of Mort's trip to the local bakery at the crack of dawn.

Too early for Roman. He'd spent a good portion of the night bringing Mort up to speed on this particular bounty. And Mort had an interesting bit of information to impart, as well. Disturbing information that Roman would have to verify before he said anything to Leah.

"I had another nightmare last night," Leah said, her expression worried.

"Tell us about it," Roman said, his gaze steady on Leah's face. Dark circles marred the delicate skin beneath her warm brown eyes and concentration lined the edges of her mouth.

He felt sorry for her. He didn't like seeing her so worn out. She'd been through so much and there was still more to come.

Leah closed her eyes, her eyebrows drawing together as she tried to recall her dream. "A house. Only not a normal house. Bigger, grander. At least it probably was at one time. In my dream it was very run-down. Dilapidated. Overgrown with bushes and wisteria. There were columns, a wide porch." She opened her eyes. "That's all."

"That's a start," Roman said, encouraged by the slow bits of memory returning.

Mort rubbed his chin with his hand. "There are a lot of old plantation homes in the South that could match that description, but the only one here in Loomis would be Renault Hall. No one's lived there for years from what I've been told." He looked at Roman. "You asked me to get the lay of the land. Let me tell y'all there are some wagging tongues in this town only too glad to spill some gossip to newcomers. Renault Hall is where Dylan Renault was murdered."

Leah's face blanched. "Dylan was…"

Roman's stomach dropped. Dread snaked through his system. She remembered the scene of Dylan's murder! The thought that maybe she *was* guilty of Dylan's death hung in the tense air around them.

Colleen reached over to take Leah's hand.

Mort drew their attention. "Originally, the sheriff accused Max Pershing of killing Renault when a land deal went south between them. But he was later released without being charged."

"Now that doesn't make a lick of sense," Colleen said. "Why would a Pershing and Renault join forces when their families have been feuding since…well, since before any of us were born?"

"Ah, so you know your Loomis history. I've been privy to all the juicy tidbits," Mort stated. "Y'all will appreciate that Ava Renault and Max Pershing are engaged. Seems the whole town's abuzz."

Colleen's gray eyes widened. "Ooh-whee, I'm sure Miz Charla's fit to be tied."

Mort's mouth quirked. "Yes, from what I understand, both the Renault and the Pershing matriarchs are not exactly jumping with joy. But Lenore Pershing went to extreme measures to break apart her son and Charla's daughter. She tried to frame Max for Dylan's murder."

Leah shook her head. "I don't think I'd want to get on the bad side of either of those two ladies."

"Well, you don't have to worry about Mrs. Pershing. She was arrested and sent to jail for trying to poison Charla Renault during the Mother of the Year Pageant last month."

"This town's a regular Peyton Place," Roman observed, not liking the penchant for gossip that seemed to permeate Loomis. Even so, the rumor mills would be a useful source for information in the next couple of days as he tried to figure out who was trying to keep Leah missing.

He captured Leah's free hand. Her bones seemed so small and crushable within his big grip. "I'd like to take you out there, to Renault Hall. See if being in the surroundings will bring back your memory."

Though she shuddered, she lifted her chin with a determined air. "I'm ready. Let's do it."

Roman appreciated and admired her bravery. "Not during daylight. Too risky, you might be seen."

"Well, y'all can't go there at night. The place is a disaster. You'd never be able to see anything," Mort interjected. "I'd suggest y'all go at the break of day tomorrow, before the good citizens of Loomis start their mornings."

"Good idea, Mort," Roman said.

"Hey, y'all didn't hire me for my good looks," Mort quipped.

Roman laughed. "True." He'd hired Mort because the man was excellent at gathering information. Roman had needed someone with anonymity. People didn't view Mort as a threat, with his congenial smile and unassuming looks. He blended in well in most situations and knew what questions to ask without stirring up suspicion.

With Roman, people took one look at him and either braced themselves for battle or turned tail and ran. Just like Leah had that first day. Just how he liked it. Normally.

"What'll we do until then?" Leah asked, drawing his attention.

"Lie low," Roman answered. "I also think it's time I inform your brother that you're alive and in town."

She bit her lower lip. "I'm not sure how I feel about that. I mean, I can't remember him."

"Maybe seeing him will jog your memory," Roman said.

"If you think it's a good idea, then call him."

Her faith in his judgment pleased him. He found Clint's number in his BlackBerry and pushed Send. A minute later, voice mail picked up. Roman didn't leave a message. Telling Clint about his sister wasn't something he wanted to do on a machine. Next, he tried Clint's office number.

The receptionist picked up. "Herald Construction."

"Clint, please."

"I'm sorry, Mr. Herald and his family are on vacation this week. Can I take a message for when he returns?" she asked, her voice cheery and friendly.

His family? Did the woman mean Sarah? Or was there someone else in the picture? "When will he return?"

"A few days." Wariness entered the woman's tone. "Was there a message?"

"No. No message." Roman hung up. "He's on vacation."

Leah's eyes widened. "He took Sarah somewhere?"

"I assume."

Leah was quiet for a moment. "That's probably good, then. At least I know she's safe with Clint."

"Yes." At least he hoped so. He chose not to mention the whole family comment to Leah. "If you need anything from town, give Mort a list."

As the ladies began making their list for Mort, Roman excused himself and took his cell phone to the parlor. He sat down on the hard, gold-and-blue brocade settee. There was a text waiting for him from Karl. Anticipation roared in his ears. He clicked open the text. His breathing quickened and adrenaline pumped through his veins as he read the words. *I think I might have a bite. I'll know within the next forty-eight hours.*

What was forty-eight hours compared to the past twenty years?

Soon, very soon, he would have a line on the man responsible for his mother's death.

FIVE

Nerves kept Leah awake most of the night, so when the first rays of dawn chased away the shadows of darkness, she was up, dressed and champing at the bit to go to Renault Hall.

Determination and desperation gnawed at her. She had to remember more, and somehow this Renault Hall was an integral part of what was locked in her brain.

She donned a pair of jeans a couple sizes too big and held them up with a leather belt. She also put on a white long-sleeved men's T-shirt that covered the mosquito bites on her arms from the swamp last night. She found a baseball cap on the top shelf of the hall closet to complete her outfit.

As she entered the kitchen, Roman offered her a Thermos full of coffee. "Good morning," he said with a smile. "Any more dreams?"

"No. I didn't sleep much." With a grateful smile, she took the container, unscrewed the cap and breathed in the strong scent of caffeine. She took a sturdy swig of the warm liquid before screwing the lid back on. Her stomach rumbled with hunger.

"You should probably eat something before we head out." He rinsed out his mug and set it on the drain board.

"I'll eat a banana on the way," she said, taking the piece of fruit from the bowl on the counter. "I need to let Grandmother Colleen know we're leaving."

"We'll be back before she's awake," Roman said, and opened the back door.

Even so, she scribbled a note in case she did awake before they returned. Leah didn't want the older woman to worry. With that done, Leah followed Roman to the truck parked out the back door.

He started up the engine. "Just in case, slump down in the seat."

She slid down until she could barely see out the front window. The banana tasted like chalk in her dry mouth. She managed to drink from the Thermos without spilling.

As the town of Loomis went by, she tried to dredge up some memory of what she was seeing. The bakery was the only place with any activity on Main Street. Leah slunk lower in the seat as they passed.

Ten minutes later, Roman brought the truck to a halt a block from Renault Hall. "We're here."

Leah sat up and gazed at the overgrown front yard of the big, dingy gray Greek Revival house. She waited for any inkling of memory, her breath stilling.

Nothing. She felt, or rather remembered, nothing.

Roman got out and came around to her door. He held out his hand. "You ready?"

Placing her hand in his, she said, "As ready as I'm going to be." He gave her hand a squeeze, and she was grateful for his steady presence as they walked toward the gated path that led to the front entrance. Nervous flutters attacked Leah. Was she really ready to find out the truth?

Roman paused at the gate and glanced around before unlatching the lock. The hinges on the black wrought iron gate squeaked as he shoved it back.

Leah preceded him into the yard. The heavy scent of decaying vegetation hung in the air. On either sides of the cracked walkway were signs of a once beautifully landscaped yard. Planter boxes overflowed with choking weeds; roses once lovingly tended had been allowed to go to seed.

What had happened that the Renaults would leave such a magnificent estate to rot away?

The stairs leading to the wide front porch were marred with moss and plants that had found their way through cracks. Roman tried the plain wooded front door, but it was locked. Leah moved to the window and peered inside the dark, empty house.

"Do you remember anything?" Roman asked, his gaze searching her face.

She shook her head with a sigh. "I don't recall ever being here."

She wandered to the edge of the porch and peered around the corner of the house. The side yard gave way to a large back area. An unkempt paved driveway curved from the main road to a structure she guessed had once been the garage. "Let's go around back," she suggested.

They fought their way through the overgrown foliage. As they entered the expanse of weedy land behind the house, Leah's gaze was drawn to a huge stone fountain that probably had once been a focal point of the landscape. At the top of the fountain, a huge brass bird tried to fly away, but its sharp talons were embedded into the stone.

Blood rushed to Leah's head. For a moment the world spun. She braced her feet apart to keep from going down.

"The bird," she whispered as shudders racked her body.

Roman's arm came around her waist, an anchor in the raging tide of her emotions. Fear gripped her, forcing her breath from her lungs. She stared at the brass bird that perhaps once had shone brightly in the sun but now had darkened with age and neglect. Its wide wings were spread, its beak hung open. The image in her nightmare.

She must have been here. Standing in this same spot, staring at the large pelican that seemed trapped in eternal fright, trying desperately to escape. Adrenaline laced with excitement grabbed her fear by the tail. This was the only solid clue so far.

"I remember this," she said, her voice shaky.

"Were you alone?"

She closed her eyes, visualizing that day. Bleakness invaded her as she related the images that flittered across the screen of her mind. "The sky had been gloomy. The bird so forlorn yet frightening in its need to escape. It made me sad. I'd been waiting." She grimaced in frustration. "I don't know why."

She tried to focus. "There was a noise from behind me." She sucked in a shocked breath as memory rushed in. "I was waiting for Dylan. But then…"

She concentrated hard on that moment. What had happened? "Pain. I remember this horrible pain." Her hand went to her head. "I was struck from behind on the head. I fell to the ground."

From there the images blurred. "There were hands pushing and pulling at me. Then…darkness."

Leah opened her eyes to stare at Roman in shock. "Do you think Dylan did this to me?"

"Maybe, but now someone else doesn't want you found."

She shivered as his ominous words took hold. "I hate this. I hate not knowing. I just wish I could remember why I was meeting Dylan. I feel like that's the key."

Roman put his hand on her shoulder, the gesture tender and comforting. "You'll remember. Look how much has already come back."

His touch brought so much comfort and strength. "True." She had to keep trying.

"We better get going before anyone sees us," Roman stated.

They were in the truck heading back to the Peel house when a thought struck Leah. "Could we go to my house? Maybe being in the place where I lived will trigger more of my memory."

Roman contemplated that idea. "You know, that's not a bad idea. We'll have to wait until dark because your apartment is right on Main Street over the pawnshop your husband owned."

Though she wasn't sure they were any closer to solving the mystery of who was out to kill her, she did feel they were making forward progress. Tonight, she prayed her mind would release the rest of the answers.

She turned to stare at the man who'd virtually crashed into her life mere days ago. With him by her side, she was confident she could face whatever she discovered.

As the evening light gave way to the shadows of the night, Roman escorted Leah to Farley's Pawn Shop in downtown Loomis. He parked the truck several blocks away. Main Street was deserted and the outline of buildings against the backdrop of the moon made Roman think of the old graphics in the comic books he enjoyed as a boy.

"What?" Leah asked.

He shifted his gaze to her. Pale light filtering in through the window revealed the worry in her brown eyes. "Excuse me?"

"Something's wrong. I can see it in your expression," she said.

"No, nothing's wrong. I was just thinking."

"About?"

"Comic books."

Her eyes widened with horrified regret. "Your collection. I'm so sorry."

He was, too. "The way the moon backlights the buildings reminds me of some of my favorite series."

"How old were you when you started reading them?"

"Eight. Discovering comics was my refuge when my mother was working. I'd retreat to the world of superheroes and crime fighters." He gave a small laugh. "Batman was my hero and Gotham City a place of adventure." He turned to look at her. "Then I discovered the comic book detective series called The Maze Agency. I couldn't get enough of them. That's when I decided one day I'd be a detective."

That dream had solidified the night his mother was attacked. Roman had confiscated the shot glass with the rapist's fingerprints, just as Jennifer Mays, the main character in the comic, had done in one issue.

He'd kept that glass in a plastic bag for years, waiting for the day he could join the police force and run the prints. That was ten years ago and still no hits.

But he wasn't ever going to give up. One day the man who'd driven his mother to commit suicide would be made to pay.

"Come on, let's get this done," he said.

They left the vehicle and rushed from one darkened doorway to another.

Leah clutched his shirt as they darted into the shadowed overhang of an office building.

"There," she whispered, and pointed across the street to the brick building. Across the front window he could barely make out the words Farley's Pawn Shop.

"That's it," he confirmed. "Wait here while I make sure all's clear."

She refused to let go of his shirt. "Don't leave me."

Her palpable fear clutched at his chest. "I'll only be a moment," he reassured her. "Trust me."

"I do," she replied, and released his shirt. "Hurry."

Her trust both pleased and scared him. He peeled away from the door and hustled across the street. He moved stealthily around to the back of the building. The back door was locked, as well, but easily picked. Carefully, he entered. Using the small handheld flashlight he'd brought, Roman took a quick survey to assure himself the place was deserted.

But after six months, he had heard the crimes were not high priority for the local sheriff, and from what he'd learned through Clint, the FBI had pulled their people and were working the unsolved murders from New Orleans.

Satisfied that it was safe for Leah to enter, he went back across the street to get her. "All clear," he said.

She pointed to the plaque on the wall next to the door that read Jocelyn Pierce, Child Psychologist.

"Yeah?" he questioned.

"Her name. I've seen it before."

His pulse quickened. "You remember her?"

Leah scrunched up her face. "I…I don't know. Do you think my brother, Clint, would have taken Sarah to see Dr. Pierce for help? I mean, this doctor was our neighbor. My daughter would have known her and maybe trusted her," she said in a whisper full of angst. "*I* would have known her."

Her vulnerability and desire to push for the truth moved him. He touched her shoulder in an attempt to comfort her. "I don't know. Maybe. I'll find out tomorrow."

She took his hand and squeezed it. "Thank you."

"Come on, before someone sees us," he said, and urged her to walk slowly, just a couple out for a midnight stroll.

They moved past the front door and dashed around the corner to the back. He led her inside and kept his flashlight aimed at the floor so the beam of light wouldn't shine through the front window.

Tentatively, Leah walked forward, her hands skimming over the counter that used to be full of jewelry. "He was found here, wasn't he?"

"Yes. On the floor in his office."

She stepped into the office and stood on the spot where her husband died and shuddered as she tried to recall the scene. Nothing surfaced, and she had to admit to herself she was thankful. "They thought he committed suicide, right?"

"At first glance. The forensic evidence says otherwise. Only his prints were on the shotgun, but the angle of the blast couldn't have been self-inflicted," Roman said softly.

Leah walked back into the main area of the store. "I don't remember this place."

Trauma. So much trauma here. But had she simply witnessed or been an active part…?

"Let's try your apartment upstairs," Roman suggested.

Her apartment. "Yes. That would be…" She hesitated. Helpful? Heartbreaking?

Steeling herself, she followed Roman up the stairs at the back of the shop. On the top landing, he paused and fiddled with the doorknob. Amused, she realized he'd picked the lock. "Another interesting skill," she murmured.

The charm of his smile in the flashlight's beam almost made her forget where they were and why. Almost.

The door swung open. Light from the moon and the streetlamp outside flooded the interior, revealing a small living space with a serviceable couch, coffee table and two plush chairs arranged for maximum viewing advantage of the wide-screen TV in the corner. The sight of several toys lying haphazardly around, as if Sarah would be back any moment to play with them, clutched at Leah's heart and made her pulse pound at her temples. Her poor baby didn't even have her toys with her.

As she ventured farther into what once had been her home, she tried to calm her racing heart and open herself to memory. She picked up a picture of her wedding day and angled the frame to take advantage of the light from outside coming through the open curtained window.

In the photo she looked happy standing next to the tall, dark-haired man. The man who was a stranger to her now. The man who was dead now.

Returning the framed photo to the side table, she walked toward the hall, instinctively knowing the bedrooms were behind the closed doors. She was aware of Roman trailing her, his presence a comfort.

Pushing open the first door, she felt tears spring to her eyes, and she sighed at their inevitability. Sarah's room. The glow of the streetlight from the window spilled across the frilly bed overflowing with stuffed animals and dolls. Though the room smelled musty, there was a lingering scent that tantalized her senses. On the dresser top she found a bottle of baby lotion. She sniffed the lotion and closed her eyes, trying to force some memory.

Nothing. Absolutely nothing. A drum solo of frustration pounded at her temples.

She abruptly turned away and found herself colliding with Roman. His arms encircled her. She rested her forehead against his chest, soaking in his support. After a moment, she pulled away, determined to continue. Something had to surface. It just had to.

She proceeded to the next room. The bedroom she'd shared with Earl.

The dark quilt on the bed was neatly made. The dark dresser against the wall was organized and tidy. She moved to the walk-in closet and flipped on the light.

"Hey," Roman exclaimed, and hustled to the window to draw the curtain. "Tell me before you do that again."

"Sorry," she muttered, her attention on the clothes hanging on either side. Men's clothes on the left and women's, apparently hers, on the right. She fingered the fabrics of the dresses and blouses, thinking maybe she could remember wearing them. But, no.

She turned her attention to Earl's clothing. A row of button-down shirts lined the top rack. Pressed slacks hung over wooden hangers on the bottom bar. She stepped closer. A scent hung on the clothes. His aftershave. She breathed deep and closed her eyes. A flash seared her mind.

Her breath came fast and labored. She recoiled from the memory that made her head pound until she thought it would explode.

She had to get out of there. She stumbled back from the closet and blindly ran out of the bedroom, across the apartment and down the stairs. Once she broke free of the building, she kept running until strong arms captured her and lifted her against a solid wall of chest.

From what seemed like a great distance, Roman's voice beckoned to her. She fought to find him in the chaos going on in her brain. She wanted Roman, not this…ugliness twisting in her mind.

"Whoa, Leah, wait, calm down. You're all right." Roman's voice broke through.

Her gaze fastened on him. She breathed in his unique scent, allowing the memories assaulting her to dissipate. She collapsed into the reassuring comfort of his hold, her legs buckling and her head falling forward so that her cheek rested against his heart as he kept her upright.

Easily lifting her into his arms, he carried her away from the pawnshop toward the park a block away. He sat on a bench beneath a live oak tree and settled her beside him. She clung to him as the pain in her mind receded.

His arms felt so protective and comforting wrapped around her, offering security and reassurance. He pressed a kiss against her temple and murmured soothing words. She arched toward him, wanting more of his attention like a flower stretches to the healing warmth of the sun.

She tilted her face upward and met his lips in a tender caress. She could feel his surprise, but she refused to release him. She needed his strength, his honor, to banish the horrors living in her mind.

He relented and deepened the kiss, offering her what she sought. Then slowly, inevitably, he withdrew his lips and dropped his forehead against hers as his chest heaved with labored breath, as if he'd just run a mile rather than merely kissed her.

Hope streaked through her, and she quickly tamped it down.

Yes, she trusted this man. Yes, she appreciated all he was doing for her, and yes, she was hugely attracted to him. But she could not allow herself to fall for him when she knew he could easily break her heart.

He believed her innocent now, but she still feared when push came to shove, he'd hand her over to the police if it meant justice would be served.

She shifted to rest her head on his shoulder. "I remembered something. Something awful."

"I gathered that by the way you bolted," he said, his tone husky.

She closed her eyes. "Earl and I were in the walk-in closet. He was so angry. He was yelling. He grabbed me by the arms, his fingers digging into my flesh. Then he hit me, calling me awful names. He said something about shaking down Dylan Renault."

"Shaking down? That sounds like he had something to blackmail Dylan with," Roman said, his voice carrying a sharp edge.

Leah sighed and lifted her head. "Yes, it does. But what, I don't know."

Frankly, she was afraid to find out.

Roman's arm tightened around Leah as he tried to reason out the last few moments. She'd remembered something important.

She'd kissed him.

And he'd kissed her back. Idiot that he was, he couldn't have denied her even if he'd tried. But the truth was he'd wanted to kiss her almost since he met her.

He wanted to again.

No, not a good idea, he mentally chastised himself. Get back to the situation at hand. Earl Farley knew something worthy of blackmail about Dylan Renault. Had Dylan killed Earl in an attempt to keep him quiet and staged Earl's death to look like a suicide?

If so, then who killed Dylan?

Despite his growing feelings for Leah, suspicion gathered on the fringes of Roman's thoughts as his gaze searched her face. Had Leah been in on the blackmail? Had she tried to continue with the scheme after her husband's death, then ended up killing Dylan in retaliation?

Then who would be after Leah now? Was there a third person in on the blackmail?

His whole being rebelled at the thought that Leah had been involved in either of the deaths. But was the rapidly expanding attraction and affection for her in his heart making him want to believe in her innocence? Had he let his guard down too much?

Yes, he had. He'd lost focus. Kissing her only served to remind him how dangerous a game he was playing. He had no intention of letting himself fall prey to the feelings bouncing around his head and his heart. Justice had to be pursued to its end. Whatever that may be.

Finding out who really killed Earl and Dylan and now wanted Leah dead was of the utmost importance. Keeping that goal in the forefront of his mind was paramount. No matter what his growing feelings for Leah were.

"Come on. We should get back to the Peel house before we're seen," he said as he rose from the bench.

Leah placed her hand in his as she stood. He tried not to notice how nicely it fit within his or how her touch made him fully aware of her.

They walked in silence through the park toward where he'd parked the truck. They entered an unlit side alley that would lead them directly to their vehicle, when a deeper shadow moved against the building. Roman halted, pulling Leah behind him.

A man slowly rose from where he'd been sitting on the stoop of a shop's side door.

"Can you spare some change?" a gravelly voice asked.

The stench of alcohol wafted on the humid air. A drunk. Roman relaxed slightly and continued walking with Leah at his heel. "No."

They passed the wobbly man, who followed closely behind. They had just reached the other end of the alley, when the moon's light illuminated them and the drunk gasped, "Oh, no!"

Roman swung around. The drunk was now visible, as well. His hair stuck up in all directions and his clothing hung off his thin frame, but it was the way the guy's face, craggy from too much drink and exposure, grimaced in fear and panic as he stared at Leah that made Roman step forward to grab the man by the arm.

"Who are you?"

The man tried to shake off Roman's grip. "No, please, no. She'll kill me."

"Who?" Roman couldn't ignore that fact that the drunk's gaze never left Leah. "Who will kill you?"

The drunk's gaze swung to Roman. "If I say anything, she'll kill me, too. Just like she did the others. Please, please, let me go. I need protection." His glassy-eyed gaze shifted back to Leah. "I'm sorry. So sorry."

Leah moved closer, confusion clear in her dark eyes. "Do I know you?"

"Please, please, let me go," the drunk whimpered, and struggled to get away from Roman.

"No one's going to hurt you," Roman said, his voice low and soothing. "Tell me who you're talking about."

"I can't," he whispered.

Gesturing to Leah, Roman asked, "Do you mean her? Has she threatened you?"

The drunk shook his head. "The lady with red hair. She'll kill me just like she did Angelina."

"Angelina?" Leah repeated the name. She grabbed Roman's arm. "The other murder victim. I remember her."

A jolt of anticipation rocked through Roman. "You do?"

From somewhere down the street, the sound of an engine turning over echoed in the quiet night. Roman's attention swung in the direction of the sound just as the drunken man yanked free of his grasp and ran back down the alley to disappear into the dark night.

"Let's go," Roman said, and hustled Leah to the street.

As they crossed the road, a car peeled away from the curb with squealing tires and bore down on them. Roman pushed Leah aside seconds before the red sports car roared past.

The same car that had been after them before.

As the car braked at the corner, the license plate glowed red in the taillights as the car zipped away.

Hurrying to where Leah had landed in a heap, Roman helped her up. "Are you hurt?"

"A little skinned up." Her voice shook. "How did he find us?"

"I don't know, but I got the plate number."

"That's good, right?"

"Yeah, it's good." He hustled Leah into the truck.

Leaving the lights off and keeping a vigilant eye out for the sports car, Roman drove down Main Street and toward the Peel house. "What about this Angelina woman?"

Ducking low so as not to be seen, Leah said, "We read an article that she'd been murdered and her body found in the swamp. But when that man said her name, something flashed in my mind. I could picture her and me, and I remember we were arguing but... Ugh, I can't recall why." She pounded the seat with her fist. "This is so frustrating. All these bits and pieces but nothing adding up to a clear picture."

He reached over and covered her fist with his hand. "It will come in time."

"Yeah, if I'm not murdered first."

Anxiety hit Roman squarely in the gut. "I'm not going to let anyone hurt you."

He only hoped they would have enough time to solve this mystery before the police figured out Leah was in town and that Roman was hiding her. Protecting her was serving justice; keeping her out of jail and alive was the only option to uncover the truth behind the murders. The risk to himself was worth the price if justice would be served.

But deep inside a little voice warned that the price he'd pay might be not only his career, but also his heart.

SIX

The next morning, Roman left early to pay the local sheriff a visit. Taking precautions not to be recognized by their would-be assailants, he changed from his normal attire and instead borrowed clothes from the bedroom closet, clothes left behind for obvious reasons, in his opinion. The loud Bermuda shorts, tourist T-shirt with the name of a local swamp tour company blazoned across the front, baseball cap and sunglasses virtually guaranteed he wouldn't be recognized by whoever was after Leah. *So* not his style.

Last night he'd sent his ex-partner on the Baton Rouge police department the license number of the red sports car. Roman expected information to be forthcoming. And then he'd pay a little visit to the driver.

But for now, his visit to the sheriff required his attention.

The old sheriff's station house stood on the corner just down the street from the Loomis Christian Church. In keeping with the town's motif, the station house was a square brick building with white-trimmed windows.

The American flag and the state of Louisiana flag flew from posts out front.

Roman pushed through the outer double doors. Cool air blasted him in the face. Roman's T-shirt, wet from the humid air outside, cooled and stuck to his back. He made his way to the desk sergeant and asked for Sheriff Reed. Within a few minutes, Roman was shown into a glass-walled office where Sheriff Bradford Reed sat behind a wide oak desk.

The sheriff tipped back in his chair and spat tobacco into a small can. "What can I do for y'all?"

Roman had debated how best to play this and decided that going in with as much of the truth as possible would better serve his purposes. "Name's Roman Black. I'm a bounty hunter hired by Dennis Farley, Earl Farley's brother, to track down Earl's killer."

Sheriff Reed's gray eyes stared at him from beneath his heavy brows. "A bounty hunter. You don't say." His gaze narrowed. "Seems I remember you from years back. You grew up here in Loomis, didn't y'all?"

Not surprised that the sheriff remembered him from his rebellious teenage days, Roman inclined his head. "That's right, Sheriff. I'd like to ask you some questions about the recent murders that have taken place here."

"Thought you said you was hired to find Farely's murderer. What's the interest in the other deaths?"

"I was hoping you could tell me if the deaths were connected."

Sheriff Reed shrugged his wide shoulders. "Could be. Maybe not. We're still working every angle."

"What do you know about the red-haired woman?"

A small tic appeared near the sheriff's eye. "What red-haired woman would that be?"

"I've been told that a red-haired woman was seen at one of the crime scenes," Roman stated, stretching the drunk's words slightly.

Sheriff Reed sat up. "Where did you hear this?"

"An anonymous tip. Do you think this red-haired woman could be behind Earl's death?"

Reed stood. His paunch butted up against the edge of his desk. "I think y'all best leave this investigation to the authorities, Mr. Bounty Hunter."

Interesting reaction. Defensive or hiding something? "Do you know of any reason why Earl Farley would have blackmailed Dylan Renault?"

The sheriff scratched his chin, and his eyes narrowed to slits. "Like I said, y'all best leave this alone." Warning echoed in the sheriff's voice.

Had Roman made a tactical error in revealing himself to the sheriff? Was the sheriff himself behind Leah's disappearance? Time for Roman to retreat and rethink his strategy. Maybe calling the FBI would be a wise decision.

Reed came around the desk and motioned for Roman to leave his office. Careful to keep his face hidden beneath his baseball cap, Roman passed through the station and made eye contact with one deputy in particular, Roman's contact within the Loomis department. The deputy gave a small nod of acknowledgment, and Roman continued on his way out the door. Once he was outside, the humid air reclaimed him and the sweet smell of the jasmine growing along the sidewalk filled his senses.

He slowly walked down the street toward the church, his posture slouched slightly and head down. The sheriff was stonewalling him. Because he was territorial about the case or because he was part of the problem? Rumor had it the sheriff was lazy, just wanted to retire. But there had definitely been a re-action to the mention of the red-haired woman. An investigation into the sheriff was definitely needed. Roman's friend Karl would be able to pick apart Sheriff Reed's life and see if the man was dirty.

Just as Roman reached for his BlackBerry to e-mail Karl with the request, the device buzzed at his waist, letting him know he had an incoming text. He glanced at the ID. Deputy Olsen texted that he'd meet Roman inside the church in fifteen minutes. Roman continued walking toward the church's side entrance.

Remembering that he'd told Leah he would ask Clint about Dr. Pierce, he tried Clint's cell phone. The voice mail picked up. He quickly left a message for Clint to call him.

Behind the church, a playground surrounded by a wooden fence marked the boundaries of the Loomis Preschool and Daycare area. No children were out in the yard at the moment.

The church's redbrick structure with its white-trimmed arched windows and steepled bell tower hadn't changed a bit since he lived in town. Not that he'd attended services. He hadn't much believed in God back then, but now he did. Earl's brother, Dennis, was a man of strong faith, and he had helped Roman find the truth in the Bible that God loved him. And Leah was helping him feel God's presence by her quiet faith.

Roman glanced around to reassure himself he wasn't being watched before entering the church. Thankfully, the town wasn't too busy on this already-hot late morning, and the few people braving the heat paid him no mind.

The cool interior smelled of lemon polish and candle wax. The wooden pews lined the red carpeted aisle that led to the altar. Roman slipped into the back corner pew. Since he had a few moments, he closed his eyes and silently prayed for not only guidance, protection and success in finding the truth about the tragedy Leah was embroiled in but also for success in finding the man who had hurt his mother. All he wanted was peace—peace and justice.

The door to the sanctuary opened and Deputy Olsen slipped inside and sat beside Roman. "I couldn't get the file," Olsen said, his voice low. "Sheriff's got it under lock and key since Mrs. Renault has been by almost every day demanding to know what's being done to find her son's killer."

"I'll bet." Roman would have liked to have seen the official report so he could get a better idea of how the investigation was proceeding. "Tell me about the sheriff. Do you think he could be involved in these deaths?"

Olsen's eyebrows rose. He let out a scoff. "Bradford can barely get out of his own way. He may be a bit of a buffoon, but he's not a murderer. Besides, he's so close to retirement, I doubt he'd do anything to screw that up."

Roman wasn't convinced, but he let it go for now. "So what *can* you tell me?"

"Not much more than I already have. As I said, the mucky mucks are keeping things pretty close to the vest."

"What do you know about the red-haired woman?"

Olsen's eyebrows rose, and he peered down his thin nose at Roman. "How do you know about the red hair?"

Deciding to keep his own information close, he shrugged. "Just heard a rumor."

Olsen snorted. "This town. I tell ya what. Gossip and rumors abound without any regard to propriety."

"It's Loomis," Roman replied in an attempt to explain the less-than-favorable behavior of its residents.

"Right." Olsen shook his head in disgust. "There were red fibers found at both the Earl Farley and Dylan Renault crime scenes. At first, the fibers appeared to be strands of long red hair, but according to the FBI's forensic team, they believe they may have come from a wig rather than from an actual head, even though the fibers were human. But—" Olsen lifted a shoulder "—that hasn't helped solve the cases."

"Any witnesses to any of the deaths?"

Olsen shook his head. "Not a one. Whoever is doing this is very clever."

Roman's heart rate picked up speed. Maybe not clever enough, because there was a witness.

The town drunk.

Now all Roman had to do was find him and make him talk.

Roman contemplated revealing this information to Deputy Olsen but decided he wanted to have a chance to question the witness before he handed him over to the sheriff's department. Roman rose. "Thanks for the info, man. I appreciate it."

Olsen held up a hand. "One thing. You might want to talk with Leah Farley's friend, the librarian, Shelby Mason."

Roman sat back down. "Thought you said there were no witnesses."

"She's not a witness to the murders, but she had some interesting things to say that would definitely give Leah Farley motive to kill her husband and Dylan Renault."

Feeling as if he'd just been hit with a sledgehammer to the chest, Roman said, "Tell me."

"She reported that she and Leah were drugged during a Renault Christmas party—"

A door near the altar opened and the pastor walked out.

"She'll have to tell you the rest." Olsen rose and quietly slipped out of the church.

Dread seized Roman's gut. Seemed there was one more person in this town Roman needed to find. The local librarian had a tale to tell.

One that could put Leah behind bars.

Imprisoned by their need for secrecy, Leah sat inside the shuttered and stifling-hot Peel house on the hard blue-and-gold living-room settee, trying desperately to remember something, anything. But nothing pierced the black void she used to be grateful for.

There had to be a way for her to remember what went on before she'd been kidnapped and left in that ditch. She needed help.

She stilled. That was the answer. Professional help.

What was the name of the doctor on the wall plaque by the office last night? Price? No, that wasn't it, but close. Pierce. Yes.

Jocelyn Pierce. Why was her name so familiar? Had they only been neighbors, or had they been friends?

Leah needed a phone book. She searched through the drawers in the kitchen and the sideboard in the hall. Finally, she unearthed a thick phone book on the top shelf of the hall closet. She quickly flipped to the white pages and found the number for Dr. Jocelyn Pierce, child psychologist.

Leah wrote her number down and prayed she could trust this woman.

She contemplated calling the counselor now but decided she'd wait for Roman to return. She didn't want to break his trust by revealing her presence in Loomis without his agreement.

To keep herself busy, she spent the next hour cleaning the house while listening to Colleen read stories from the various magazines that Mort had brought home from the store. As she mopped the kitchen floor, it came to her where she'd read Jocelyn's name. Dr. Pierce had been the woman quoted in an article Leah had read. Jocelyn had called Leah her friend. Surely, she'd help Leah now.

When Roman finally returned, Leah immediately told him her idea of seeing the psychologist and of the doctor's statement in the paper.

His expression turned thoughtful. "Might be a good idea. We'd have to figure out a way to get you there without being seen. Our friend in the sports car could be anyone or anywhere."

A shiver of apprehension skated over her skin. She couldn't forget last night's near miss. Whoever was after her had been staking out the pawnshop. Would they be watching the doctor's office, as well? It was a risk she was willing to take.

"What did you learn while you were out?" she asked, wrapping her arms around her middle.

"Enough to know we need to find that bum and question him," he replied.

"Were you able to talk with Clint? Is Sarah seeing Dr. Pierce?"

"I left him a message." He indicated the sideboard where the phone sat. "You should make the call."

Leah swallowed back the sudden trepidation clogging her throat. What would she say? *Hi, I'm an accused murderer and need help remembering if I really killed my husband so I'll know if I can ever return to my child?* Should go over real well.

She reached for the phone and dialed.

A woman answered. "Dr. Pierce."

Leah cleared her throat. "Yes, um…" Should she reveal herself so quickly? "I'd like to make an appointment."

"Have you been seen by this office before?"

Leah frowned, concentrating on the doctor's voice. If only she could remember how close they were. Leah could only hope some memories would rise up once she and the doctor were face-to-face. "No. I'd be a new patient. I think."

Dr. Pierce gave a small laugh. "You think?"

Leah smiled, already liking the warmth in the other woman's tone. "No, I know. I'd be a new patient. Do you have time to see me this afternoon?"

"Yes, I do. Though, you realize I specialize in children?"

"I do." She latched on to the simplest excuse available to her. "But there doesn't seem to be any other psychologist in town."

Would this woman really be able to help her, or was she grasping at straws? More important, was this doctor helping her daughter?

"True. Could you come to my office at two this afternoon?"

"Two o'clock?" Leah looked to Roman for confirmation of the time. It only gave them an hour to prepare. He nodded. "Yes, two would work," Leah said into the phone.

"Wonderful. And your name?"

Leah hesitated. They'd been friends once, or so the woman had been quoted saying. Leah prayed their friendship would stand the test of this mess. But she wasn't going to take any chances. Not over the phone. If Jocelyn recognized her when she arrived, at least Leah would have time to beg for her cooperation. "Abigail. Abigail Lang."

"I look forward to working with you, Abigail."

Leah hung up and began to shake. Roman's hands came to rest on her shoulders. "You okay?"

She turned and wrapped her arms around his solid frame, feeling as if she were clinging to the only anchor left in the storm she'd found herself in. He held her stiffly, nothing like he had the night before when he'd allowed her to kiss him and kissed her back.

Confused by his aloofness, she drew away enough to stare into his face, noting the hard lines around his mouth and the detachment in his cool gaze. She couldn't help the spurt of disappointment when he let go and stepped back, putting more distance between them.

"I have to talk with Mort. Be ready to go about twenty to two," he said, and left her standing in the middle of the parlor, feeling alone and insecure about the future.

After filling Mort in on the information Olsen had supplied and giving him instructions to track down the drunk from the alley, Roman made a phone call to the local library. Once he had the information he needed, he debated changing into more appropriate attire for interviewing a witness. Dressing all in black held a certain amount of intimidation that Roman found useful. He decided to stay with his disguise. Looking like a tourist wouldn't garner nearly the attention his black ensemble would.

He found Leah in the kitchen with Colleen. They were sharing a sandwich and soda.

He waved off her offer of food. "We should get going. Mort will drive us into town."

She cleared away her plate and put on a hat and a pair of dark, round sunglasses. "What do y'all think of my disguise?"

"Very nice." He had to admit she didn't look anything like the waif he'd first encountered. She'd slicked all of her short curls back and tucked them under the wide-brimmed straw hat perched on her head. She wore a long-sleeved blouse buttoned to the chin beneath overalls that hid every curve and angle of her slender frame. He hoped the disguise worked.

With Mort at the wheel of the truck, Roman slouched down in the passenger seat and really looked at the town. Flat-roofed, brick buildings lined one side of Main Street. Near the middle of town an inviting park stretched for at least a mile. Tall live oaks and pines draped with Spanish moss dotted the park, providing some shaded relief from the heat.

A picturesque gazebo stood near the center like a grand old lady holding court. Just past the park were more brick buildings and at the corner, the pawnshop, with Dr. Pierce's office across the street.

Roman twisted in the seat to search Leah's face. "Are you ready for this?"

Though she looked terrified, she nodded. A wave of admiration washed over him and warred with the suspicions Olsen had aroused. Leah certainly didn't lack backbone.

"Mort, circle back around so she can get out right in front of the office." He didn't want her walking around where she might bump into someone who could see past the disguise.

Mort went around the block and then brought the truck to a halt directly in front of Dr. Pierce's office door. Roman climbed out and helped Leah out of the cab. He held her hand for a moment, wishing he could reassure her that she'd be fine, that she wasn't a murderer. But he just wasn't so sure anymore himself.

Leah entered the office with her heart in her throat. *Please, Lord, don't let me be making a mistake.*

The small outer waiting room was empty and the door to the doctor's office closed. Keeping her disguise in place, Leah poured herself a cup of water from the pitcher on the mahogany sideboard. Her hand shook as she lifted the cup to her mouth. The cool liquid slid down and she savored the sensation. Behind her, the doctor's-office door opened. Leah braced herself for this encounter with a stranger as she turned. Even through the dark lenses of her sunglasses, she could see that the tall, slender woman standing in the doorway was beautiful, with dark blond hair and compassionate blue eyes.

Jocelyn Pierce smiled, showing pretty white teeth. "You must be Abigail." She came forward with her hand outstretched.

Leah tried to swallow, but her mouth had gone dry despite the water she'd drank. Something in the deep recesses of her mind stirred, and Leah wasn't sure if she should be afraid or relieved. Politeness required she shake the doctor's hand, but all Leah wanted to do was turn and run.

"Thank you for seeing me," Leah managed to say.

"Please, come in." Dr. Pierce indicated the other room. "I have a few forms for you to fill out."

Leah followed the doctor into a beautifully appointed office where medical degrees dominated one

Here's great news for fans
of inspirational fiction:

novels are now available
in different series!

2 FREE
Love Inspired® Romance
113-IDL-EXCY
313-IDL-EXDY

2 FREE
Love Inspired® Suspense
123-IDL-EXDC
323-IDL-EXEC

2 FREE
Love Inspired® Historical
102-IDL-EXDN
302-IDL-EXEN

*Place one
sticker
on the
reply card
inside.*

**Use one of these
peel-off stickers to get**

2 FREE
BOOKS

in the series you like best!

Romance? Suspense? Historical? The choice is yours!

Whether you prefer heartwarming romance, spine-tingling suspense or action-packed historical fiction, now you can find *Love Inspired®* novels to suit your taste and interests! And whichever series you choose, you can be sure that the books feature traditional conservative values, with themes of faith and the redemptive power of love.

Please allow us to send you two free books in the series you prefer. You're under no obligation to purchase anything. We hope you'll want to continue receiving them—always at a discount price and before they're available in bookstores—but that's entirely up to you.

Love Inspired® Romance
You'll enjoy these contemporary inspirational romances with Christian characters facing the challenges of today's world.

Love Inspired® Suspense
You'll be thrilled by these contemporary tales of intrigue and romance as the characters confront challenges to their faith ... and to their lives!

Love Inspired® Historical
With themes of romance, adventure and faith, these historical stories will sweep you away to another time and another world.

Order online at:
www.LoveInspiredBooks.com

Along with your FREE BOOKS you'll also get **TWO FREE MYSTERY GIFTS!** We can't tell you what they are – that would spoil the surprise – but they're worth about $10!

For novels in which family, faith and the redemptive power of love are central themes, return the reply card today!

WHICH FREE BOOKS SHOULD WE SEND YOU?

Affix one peel-off sticker (from the front of this insert) to indicate which series of *Love Inspired®* novels you'd prefer. We'll send you two free books in the series you select, and we'll also send you two free mystery gifts.

Accepting these books and gifts places you under no obligation to purchase anything, ever.

```
PLACE PEEL-OFF STICKER HERE
```

FIRST NAME   LAST NAME

ADDRESS

APT #   CITY

STATE/PROV.   ZIP/POSTAL CODE

Offer limited to one per household. Offer not applicable towards series that subscriber is currently receiving. Please allow 4 to 6 weeks for delivery. Offer available while quantities last. **Your Privacy**–Steeple Hill Books is committed to protecting your privacy. Our Privacy Policy is available online at www.SteepleHill.com or upon request from the Steeple Hill Reader Service. From time to time we make our lists of customers available to reputable third parties who may have a product or service of interest to you. If you would prefer for us not to share your name and address, please check here ☐.

◄ DETACH AND MAIL – POSTAGE HAS BEEN PAID ►

® and ™ are trademarks owned and used by the trademark owner and/or its licensee.

LI-3P-09

Printed in the U.S.A.
© 2008 Steeple Hill Books

Steeple Hill Reader Service — Here's how it works:

Accepting your 2 free books and 2 free mystery gifts places you under no obligation to buy anything. You may keep the books and gifts and return the shipping statement marked "cancel." If you do not cancel, about a month later we'll send you 4 more books and bill you just $4.24 each (U.S.) or $4.74 each (Canada). That's a savings of at least 20% off the cover price, that's quite a bargain! Shipping and handling is just 25 cents per book, along with any applicable taxes.* You may cancel at any time, but if you choose to continue, every month we'll send you 4 more books, which you may either purchase at the discount price or return to us and cancel your subscription. **NOTE: *Love Inspired* *Historical* books are published bi-monthly and will be shipped EVERY OTHER month.**

*Terms and prices subject to change without notice. Sales tax applicable in N.Y. Canadian residents will be charged applicable provincial taxes and GST. Offer not valid in Quebec. All orders subject to approval. Credit or debit balances in a customer's account(s) may be offset by any other outstanding balance owed by or to the customer.

If offer card is missing write to: Steeple Hill Reader Service, P.O. Box 1867, Buffalo, NY 14240-1867

BUSINESS REPLY MAIL

FIRST-CLASS MAIL   PERMIT NO. 717   BUFFALO, NY

POSTAGE WILL BE PAID BY ADDRESSEE

STEEPLE HILL READER SERVICE
PO BOX 1867
BUFFALO NY 14240-9952

NO POSTAGE
NECESSARY
IF MAILED
IN THE
UNITED STATES

wall. In the corner, a toy box overflowing with dolls and Tonka trucks waited to be played with. Had Sarah played here while the doctor tried to help her understand her mommy's disappearance? Leah's heart ached at the thought.

Leah took the offered forms from the doctor and sat in the leather chair facing the desk. A picture of the doctor and a very handsome man sat at an angle on the desktop so that occupants on both sides of the mahogany desk could view the framed photo. Leah dropped her gaze to the forms but didn't write anything.

"Would you like to tell me why you're here today?"

Leah licked her lips and lifted her gaze. How did she begin to explain? "I…I need some help."

Dr. Pierce's blue eyes were vivid with curiosity. "If I can, I will. Why don't you tell me what the problem is."

Feeling suddenly ridiculous in the hat and glasses, Leah stripped both away.

Doctor Pierce gasped. "Leah?"

Her heart stalled and then jammed against her ribs. She jumped from the chair and started toward to the door. "This was a mistake."

Dr. Pierce rose. "Wait! What's going on? Leah, where have you been? I've been so worried about you. We all have."

Fearful, yet so desperate to believe her, Leah hesitated, her hand on the doorknob. "You have? Really?"

The doctor frowned and came around the desk. "Leah, tell me what's happening. Don't you know me?"

Tears gathered at the corners of Leah's eyes. She

shook her head. "No, I don't. See, that's just it. I can't remember anything."

"Oh, my," the doctor said, her eyes widening with understanding. "You have amnesia. Wow. Oh, honey."

Amazed to see tears in this woman's eyes, Leah stepped away from the door. "We were friends once, right?"

Jocelyn nodded. "Yes. Oh, Leah, I feel so awful that I wasn't here for you. You left that cryptic message on my machine and then you disappeared." She placed a hand over her heart. "I feared you were dead."

"Someone wants me dead," Leah stated, trying to stem the tears that were flowing so freely now that she had found a friend from her past.

"We have to call Sam," Jocelyn exclaimed, and moved back to her desk.

Not sure who Sam was, but sensing a threat, Leah said, "No, you can't tell anyone I'm here. Please. Trust me on this. It's too dangerous."

Jocelyn paused. "I think you need to explain to me what's going on."

"Yes, I do." Leah sat once again in the leather chair. "And I hope you can help me to regain my memory. But first, do you know how Sarah is?"

Jocelyn's face brightened. "You remember her?"

Leah shook her head. "Sadly, no."

Jocelyn sighed. "Sarah's safe. She misses you. I've been working with her, but it's so hard when they're young. Though we have discovered she's afraid of women with long red hair. All except Shelby, of course."

Leah's pulse sped up. The drunk last night had also

been afraid of a woman with red hair. Could it be the same woman? "Why is she afraid?"

"She saw something the night Earl died," Jocelyn said.

"She did?" Leah's heart constricted in her chest. She tried to remember that night, but a throbbing at her temple was her only reward. "Who's Shelby?"

"Our friend. Your best friend."

She had a best friend? More determined than ever, Leah said, "*Please,* you have to help me remember."

Jocelyn skipped her own chair and came around to sit beside Leah. She gathered her hands in hers. "I still can't believe you're here. Of course I'll help you. Tell me everything."

Leah did, starting from the moment she awoke to the moment she entered the office. Jocelyn sat back with a stunned expression on her face. "I really should call Sam."

"Who's Sam?"

Jocelyn's expression softened. "My husband. We were married a few months ago. He's with the FBI, he'll be able to protect you."

Sam Pierce. Leah recalled he was named in one of the articles she'd read. She shook her head and held tightly to Jocelyn's hand. "No. Not yet. Roman will protect me."

"But it sounds like he's in danger, too," Jocelyn said.

Her insides twisted with guilt. "Yes, he is." She pleaded with her friend. "Please, you have to help me. Is there hypnotherapy or something you can do to make my memory come back?"

"There's no magic cure, Leah. The mind is a complex organ. It sounds like you've regained some memory, and we can build on that. We'll talk through the memories that have surfaced and pray that more will rise up."

Not the quick, easy fix she was hoping for, but it felt good to have another person on her side. Would Jocelyn's husband be a supporter or would he be of the mind that she was guilty until proven innocent? "Maybe we should start with the fight Earl and I had."

Jocelyn nodded in agreement. "Good idea. Close your eyes, let your mind drift to the closet in your apartment. You're there with Earl."

Leah relaxed and tried to let the images flow. "He's so angry," Leah whispered, flinching from the memory.

"What is he saying?"

"He's cursing at me, calling me horrible names. He's accusing me of…" It was right there, yet out of reach. The names reverberated around her head, painting an ugly picture. She winced. "He thinks I've slept with someone else."

Nausea turned her stomach. Was she the type of person to cheat on her husband?

"An affair?" Surprise rang in Jocelyn's voice.

"He's in a rage. Asking how I could have deceived him all these years." The memory didn't make sense. "He says he's going to make Dylan pay. Shake him down."

"Dylan? Hmm."

Something in her tone drew Leah's attention. She opened her eyes. "What? What do you know?"

The sympathy in Jocelyn's blue eyes didn't bode well. "When Dylan died, his last words were *Sarah's father.*"

Leah heart raced in confusion. "Why would he talk about Earl at his death? Earl died before Dylan. This doesn't make sense."

"I don't think Dylan meant Earl, he meant himself. That *he* was Sarah's father," Jocelyn explained gently.

Feeling as if she had taken a punch to the solar plexus, Leah blinked. "I don't understand."

"Was Dylan Sarah's biological father?"

Leah broke out in a sweat. The room spun. She yanked her hands from Jocelyn's to grip the armrests of the chair. Dylan. Sarah. Biological. No. No, no, no.

Her breathing came fast and shallow. From a long distance she could hear the concern in Jocelyn's voice but her words wouldn't compute. Dylan. Sarah's father.

Earl's words made sense now. She understood why he'd called her those awful names and why he'd accused her of lying to him. He wasn't Sarah's father, and he'd somehow found out.

But he didn't understand. She'd hadn't had an affair with Dylan.

She remembered now.

Dylan had raped her.

And she didn't want anyone to know.

SEVEN

The Loomis library parking lot was nearly full when Roman pulled the truck into a space after he'd dropped Mort off downtown with instructions to see if any of the locals knew the whereabouts of the man he had now discovered from Deputy Olsen was Chuck Peters, the town drunk.

The lush lawn surrounding the library sported stone benches beneath flowering dogwood trees. Roman headed toward the stone steps leading to the entrance of the large brick building. Through the high arched windows, shelves brimming with books were visible. Not much had changed on the outside since he was a kid.

He entered the building and noted that the inside seemed brighter and the red carpet beneath his boots looked new. He went directly to the circulation desk. The gray-haired woman behind the counter smiled at him. The badge she wore said her name was Miss Maynard. "Do you need a library card, young man?"

"No, I'm actually here to see Shelby Mason. Is she available?"

The woman's eyebrows rose. "She's in the reference section upstairs. Are you a relative?"

Roman forced a polite smile. "No, ma'am."

He headed up the stairs and followed the signs directing him to the reference section. A young woman with long red hair stood, stacking big volumes of books onto a cart. The red hair stopped him cold. Was the story she'd told the police about Leah only fiction to keep the focus off herself? Librarian by day, accomplice to murder by night?

Suspicion churned in his gut. He'd get to the truth soon enough. "Miss Mason?"

She straightened and stared at him in surprise. "Yes, may I help you?"

"I hope so." He held out his hand. "My name is Roman Black, and I'm investigating the deaths of Earl Farley and Dylan Renault."

She extracted her hand and her expression closed. "I don't have any more to tell you people."

Aware that she'd assumed he was with the police, Roman chose not to correct her. He walked a fine line between truth and fiction. He'd become good at not crossing it.

If the circumstances were different and he wasn't considering her an accomplice to murder, he might warn her to always ask for ID when approached by anyone claiming to be the police. But for now, her ignorance worked to his advantage.

"It's very important you cooperate, Miss Mason. Is there somewhere private that we can talk or would you rather do this here?" he said.

She gave him a measuring stare. He stared right back. She sighed. "This way."

Roman followed her to a small, glass-enclosed conference room. When the door was firmly shut, he said, "In your statement to the police, you claimed that you and Leah were both drugged during a Renault company Christmas party, is that correct?"

She pursued her lips. "Yes, that is correct."

"But you never reported it until after Dylan Renault was dead. Why is that?"

"I had no proof."

"You still don't."

"No, I don't. I just have my memory of that night."

Roman watched her eyes for any signs of lying. He didn't see any guile. "Tell me, Miss Mason, what exactly happened *that* night."

"I already told all of this to Agent Pierce," she said impatiently.

"I understand, but *I* need to hear you tell me what happened. Please, it's very important." Miss Mason's story could be the key to unlocking Leah's memory. And providing motive for murder. He suddenly had a bad case of heartburn.

"It didn't seem all that important a few months ago," she said. "Y'all still think Leah had something to do with Earl's and Dylan's death. I am sure she didn't. Leah was…*is* my best friend in the whole world. I knew her better than anyone, and I tell you she wouldn't do something so evil."

She sounded so sincere, and since neither the sheriff nor the FBI had connected Miss Mason to the crimes despite the woman's long red hair, Roman decided to appeal to her friendship with Leah. "Leah is why I'm here. She is in grave danger and any information you have could help us."

Her eyes grew wide. "You know where Leah is? She's not dead?"

The eager hopefulness in her lovely eyes gripped Roman. He wanted to assure her Leah was safe. "I'm trying to bring her home, and I need to know what happened the night of the Renault Christmas party."

Shelby put her hand to her heart. "Of course. Anything, if it will help Leah. You see, she worked for Dylan Renault. He'd been hitting on her for months. This was before she'd married Earl, not that her being married would have stopped Dylan… Anyway, Leah wasn't interested, so she'd begged me to go with her to the company party."

"Where was this party?"

"At the Renault home."

"So you went," Roman prodded.

"I did, mainly to run interference with Dylan. Dylan wasn't a man who was used to hearing *no*. At the party, he wouldn't leave Leah alone. We both were drinking ginger ale, but at one point Dylan brought us cups of punch. A little later, Leah said she felt sick and within a matter of minutes, so did I. It was very strange."

"So you think he drugged the punch?" Anger simmered in Roman's belly. Only a degenerate would stoop so low.

Shelby gave a grim nod. "Yes, I do. The room

started spinning, and I thought I was going to be sick. Someone helped me to a sofa in a quiet room."

She gave a delicate shrug of her slim shoulders. "That's the last thing I remember. I awoke the next morning still on that couch, and Leah was gone. A maid told me Dylan had taken Leah home because she wasn't feeling well. At the time, I was angry thinking she'd left me there. So I went straight to her apartment."

A lump of dread hit Roman, making any intake of air suddenly a chore. "And she told you what?"

Shelby shook her head. "She wouldn't talk about the party at all. I knew something was wrong because she wouldn't look me in the eye. She claimed she'd had a twenty-four-hour bug. I, too, felt like I'd had the flu. But Leah had bruises on her wrists and on her face. She said she'd fallen."

"But you don't believe that." Roman wanted to think she'd only fallen, but everything inside him screamed foul.

"No, I don't." Her intelligent eyes regarded him with frank honesty. "I think Dylan Renault raped her."

Hearing her say the words pierced through every conceivable argument summoned in self-defense.

Dylan had raped Leah.

The knowledge seared him all the way to his soul.

And not just because now he'd established motive.

"She quit her job the next day, which I thought was telling."

He worked to gather his composure. "So three months later, she realized she was pregnant with

Sarah." Which was in line with the town gossip Mort had heard. Sarah Farley was a Renault by blood.

Shelby bit her lip. "I don't know. I mean, I guess. Leah started seeing Earl almost immediately after that night. He'd shown interest in her for several months prior but she hadn't reciprocated the interest until a few days after the party."

Sad wistfulness entered Shelby's gaze. "She seemed really content with Earl, and I was happy for her. They were married within a few months and then announced that she was pregnant. We never spoke of the Christmas party again."

Shelby made a helpless gesture with her hand as tears gathered in her eyes. "I should have made her talk to me. I can't help but feel that if I had, somehow none of this would have happened."

Roman frowned, not sure how to console this woman. "I know Leah wouldn't want you to feel guilty."

She gave him a wan smile. "You sound as though you know her well."

Did he? Maybe. At least he had come to know the woman she was now. But the woman she had been before losing her memory?

Was that woman capable of murdering her husband and the father of her child in order to keep her secret?

If so, what was he going to do about it?

When Roman picked Leah up in front of Jocelyn's office, his marked silence made her already-knotted nerves that much more tightly bunched. She found it strange that he didn't ask how the session with the psychologist had gone.

Finally, she couldn't take the grim silence anymore. "I really liked Jocelyn. She and I were evidently good friends. And she is helping Sarah. She thinks Sarah saw something the night Earl died."

He glanced at her then. "Was she able to help you remember the night of Earl's murder?"

Leah frowned. The tone in his voice made her think he thought she was there at the scene. "I don't remember his death."

"He was angry with you," he stated.

"Yes."

"Because he found out Sarah wasn't his child," he said, his voice low, intense.

Her breath hitched. "How did you know?"

"How did Earl find out about Sarah?"

"I don't... I can't remember it all," she hedged as her heart pounded in her ears.

Would Roman think Sarah's paternity was motive enough for Leah to commit murder? Would he turn her in now?

"I talked with another friend of yours today, Shelby Mason," Roman said as he pulled the truck to the side of the road under a cypress tree.

Jocelyn had mentioned Shelby. Leah had no memory of her, but obviously they had been close if she'd told Shelby about Sarah. She swallowed. Unsure how to feel about this information, she asked, "What did she say?"

He turned to face her. "Do you remember the Renault Christmas party four years ago?"

Everything inside her recoiled, yet no specific memory surfaced, only a sense of impending doom and a deep certainty that that night must have been when Dylan raped her. But how could she voice this to Roman?

He reached out to run a finger down her cheek, capturing a tear she hadn't realized she'd shed. "What happened with Dylan?"

She shook her head. "I don't know. I can't remember."

"You can't, or you won't?"

She lifted her eyes to meet his gaze. The gentleness in his dark eyes floored her. "Maybe both."

"Is Sarah Dylan's child?"

Leah swallowed back the bile that rose. She didn't want to admit it, didn't want to go down this road. But she cared too much about Roman to lie to him. Slowly, she inclined her head. "I believe so."

"Because he raped you."

She cringed at the stark, awful words. "I only just remembered that with Jocelyn's help. Please, don't tell anyone else."

His dark eyebrows drew together. "Shelby Mason was with you at that party. She always thought that was what happened, but you would never talk about it."

So even when she did have her memory, she'd been living in denial. "Earl somehow found out. That's why he was so angry that night."

Roman searched her face. "What happened the day of Earl's death?"

"I told you, I can't remember," she pleaded. He had to understand. He had to believe her. "I wish I could."

"Leah, this changes everything," Roman said, his

voice full of regret. "I can't continue to hide you. We need to get you a good lawyer."

She closed her eyes as his meaning hit her square in the chest. She knew what he had to do…turn her over to the authorities. As much as she wanted to protest, she'd come to care for him too much to allow him to continue to sacrifice his honor and integrity by hiding her. Especially when it was clear he now thought she'd murdered two men.

Taking a bracing breath, she said, "I know. It's time for me to go to the police."

His grim expression tore at her heart. "It's the only way if you ever hope to get your daughter back."

But not if she were convicted of murder.

Roman really wanted to believe in Leah's innocence, but doubts clouded his judgment. Turning her in had been the right thing to do. No matter how painful. Justice came with a price.

But handing her over to Sheriff Bradford Reed was a toxic weed to swallow. Karl's investigation had turned up nothing that pointed to the sheriff being involved in the murders or Leah's kidnapping. But Sheriff Reed couldn't hide the gloating in his dull, yellowing eyes when they had walked by. Roman was sure the sheriff saw bringing Leah in as his crowning glory before retirement.

Thankfully, Leah had thought to call her friend, Dr. Pierce, who assured Leah that her husband, Sam, an FBI agent, would be coming in on the investigation.

At least with an outsider involved, Leah would get a fair shake. And with Dr. Pierce's testimony that Leah suffered from amnesia, the courts would have to give her the benefit of the doubt. At least, Roman prayed so.

Poor Colleen was beside herself without Leah. Aching for the older woman, Roman had made it clear that she could stay at the Peel house for as long as she wanted. Colleen had been adamant that she wasn't leaving town with Leah rotting in jail alone, which made Roman feel even worse for leaving town now.

As Roman and Mort packed up to leave, Roman couldn't quell the relentless feeling that he was abandoning Leah. He told himself he had fulfilled his commitment. He'd found the woman accused of killing Earl Farley, and soon he'd collect his money from Dennis. Then Roman's debt of honor to Dennis would be paid in full. End of story. Her guilt or innocence shouldn't be his concern.

Only he couldn't shake the knowledge that someone who was willing to kill Leah, Colleen and him was still out there. Regardless of Sheriff Reed's assurance of Leah's safety in his custody, every protective instinct inside Roman screamed a protest as he threw his stuff into the truck.

His heart squeezed painfully in his chest. He couldn't do it. He just couldn't leave Leah in jail, not when the danger still lurked. The plates on the red sports car had turned up stolen. A dead end there. And Mort hadn't been able to locate Chuck Peters—the bum who'd seen something—something that could exonerate Leah. Sheriff Reed hadn't been even remotely interested when Roman told him about the drunk's story.

There was only one other person in Loomis who would want to help clear Leah's name, and who might know where to find the bum.

Roman climbed into the truck with Mort and said, "We're going to go see Clint Herald, Leah's brother."

Clint's business was located in an old Victorian home that he'd converted into office space. The receptionist had shown Roman directly into Clint's office. The last time Roman had seen Clint he'd informed him he was going to find Earl Farley's murderer. Clint's sister.

At the time Roman had been sure Leah was guilty. Now he wasn't sure. Not sure at all. His heart told him she wouldn't do something so evil, yet a nagging doubt lingered. Roman didn't know the woman she'd been, only the woman she was now. And wasn't that what mattered? The question really was, were they the same woman?

"You found my sister and you turned her over to the sheriff?" Clint Herald's outrage made the cords along the column of his neck taut as he rounded the corner of his desk. Though older than his sister, Clint had the same dark hair and eyes. The family resemblance between the siblings was strong.

Roman held up his hand. "I arranged for her to have

the best lawyer in Baton Rouge. Clive Gerade is on his way down as we speak."

"I can't believe you didn't tell me sooner."

Roman cocked a brow. "You were on vacation. I left you a message."

Clint ran a hand through his dark hair. "I have to see her."

"There's something else you have to understand," Roman said. "She has amnesia."

"Amnesia?" Clint's stunned expression made it clear that he hadn't thought of that possibility. "So that's why she stayed away so long. I knew there had to be an explanation. Leah wouldn't just abandon Sarah. Ever." Clint strode across his office, toward the door. "I have to go see my sister."

"Wait," Roman said. "I need your help finding someone. Someone who might be able to help Leah."

Clint frowned. "You said you already hired a lawyer."

"The other night, Leah and I ran into a red-haired bum—Chuck Peters, a friend of mine—who might have information about the murders," Roman stated. "We need to find him."

"Chuck?" Clint made a face. "He's drunk so often I doubt the sheriff would take anything the man said seriously."

"You know him?"

"Yeah, I know him. The whole town knows him."

"Well, what the sheriff will or will not believe is irrelevant. All we need is someone to establish reasonable doubt in the minds of a jury, if this case ever gets that far. Believe me, I've see less scrupulous characters take the stand and sway a jury. Chuck may be Leah's only chance."

"Fine, I'll help you find Chuck—after I see Leah."

"Fair enough. Let's go."

Leah sat in the dank, muggy jail cell and struggled not to let self-pity overwhelm her. Sweat dripping from her brow mingled with her tears, and she gave them an impatient swipe. She squeezed her eyes tightly closed. "Dear God, please help me remember. If I did harm to anyone, I need to know. And if not, then please help me out of this mess."

The sound of footsteps echoed in the cement cubicle, and the ominous noise sent a ripple of fear cascading over her flesh. Then the sheriff was at the bars, followed closely by a tall, dark-haired man.

"Mrs. Farley, your brother is here to see you," the sheriff intoned with a dose of irritation.

Leah rose from the single cot and approached the bars. She studied the man staring at her with tears in his eyes. The darkness of his hair and eyes matched her own. But his sculptured face was that of a stranger.

"It's really you," he said. "I've been going out of my mind with worry."

The voice didn't even sound familiar. Her hands gripped the bars. Disappointment ran ice cold through her veins. She didn't know what to say but the truth. It hurt her heart to think she couldn't even recall her own brother. "I'm sorry. I don't remember you."

His crestfallen expression only served to hurt her more. "Is Sarah safe?" she asked.

Eager hopefulness stole across his face. "You remember her?"

She didn't realize she could hurt any worse than she already did. "No."

A pained expression crossed Clint's features. "She's safe. I've taken good care of her. I hired a wonderful woman to help me, and she's become much more than that to us now. Sarah's going to be so happy to see you," Clint said as he used the back of his hand to wipe away his tears. He visibly gathered himself. "Roman told me you have amnesia."

Her heart quickened. "You spoke with Roman?"

Clint nodded. "Yes, he's arranging for your bail."

She couldn't believe it. She'd expected that he'd be far from this dreadful town by now, already moving on to another job. But he wasn't. He was here, arranging for her bail. Tenderness welled up, choking her. He hadn't abandoned her, after all. *Thank You, Lord.*

A whirring hiss bounced off the walls and drew Leah's attention. A matronly woman draped in pearls rolled forward in an electric wheelchair, followed closely by a tall, thin man dressed in a stark black suit.

Clint's surprised and angry expression alerted Leah that this was not a friend.

"Charla Renault? You have got to be kidding me," Clint muttered. "Mrs. Renault, what are you doing here?"

The chair came to an abrupt halt beside Clint. The distinct floral scent of perfume teased Leah's nose and tickled something deep in her mind. She didn't have the time to dwell on it as Mrs. Renault turned her sharp-eyed gaze to Leah.

"I came to see for myself that—" she pointed one bony finger in Leah's direction "—this woman was truly behind bars." Charla Renault's green eyes narrowed viciously, and hatred fairly crackled in the air around the older woman. "My darling son is dead because of *you*. Make no mistake, you'll pay."

The ferociousness of her vehement words sent chills slithering down Leah's spine. Leah remained silent. Her heart beat so hard in her chest she heard the sound echo off the walls, but then Roman stalked forward and Leah realized she'd simply heard the reverberation of his footfalls as he joined Clint and Charla Renault.

He glowered at Mrs. Renault. "You need to leave."

Mrs. Renault arched a high eyebrow, obviously affronted. "No one tells me what to do. Especially not some two-bit hoodlum from the bad side of town. Roman Black," she scoffed. "You look just like your mother, and she was no good, either."

Leah's sharp intake of breath filled the small cell. From her side of the bars, she could only watch with dread as Roman's hands curled into fists. Clint stepped closer to Roman as if he thought Roman the type of man who would strike a woman. Leah knew different, even if the woman provoked violence.

"Here, now, break it up." Sheriff Reed charged into the middle of the group. "Mrs. Renault, I told you to wait for me. Bosworth, would you please see Mrs. Renault to my office?"

The man named Bosworth seemed resigned as he stepped closer. "Come along, Ms. Charla, this way."

She waved away his efforts to maneuver her chair. "Leave me be, Bosworth. I'm not a ninny you can push around." Charla turned her attention back to Leah. Her lip curled in a nasty sneer. "You'll fry for my son's death, and I can't wait."

Leah shuddered as Charla turned her chair around and motored away.

"Sheriff, unlock the door," Roman barked, his hands still fisted and his dark eyes alight with anger.

"All in good time," Sheriff Reed said. "Now listen, young lady, your bail has been posted, but you are not to leave town. No more disappearing acts."

"She was kidnapped, Sheriff." Roman ground the words out between his teeth.

Roman was sticking up for her. Warmth for this man curled through Leah.

"So she says," Reed replied, his tone echoing with disbelief as he unlocked the door. "Mind you, the FBI will be arriving soon and they want to question you both," he said before shuffling away.

Grateful to be free, Leah slipped into Roman's embrace. "Thank you."

His expression softened. "You're welcome. Let's get out of here," Roman said, and steered her toward the exit.

Clint stepped close and touched Leah's hand. She curled her fingers around his, thankful for his support even if she didn't remember him.

A few feet from the exit, Charla Renault's strident voice stopped them in their tracks.

"What do you mean, you've let her go! How dare you! I'll have your job for this, Bradford!"

"I suggest we hurry before she notices us," Clint stated dryly.

The three nodded in agreement and pushed through the station door. Once outside, Roman led them across the street into the park and stopped at a picnic table.

The lush green lawn that made up the majority of the park was full of children out of school for the summer. The merry laughter filled the air and lessened the tenseness of Leah's nerves.

Clint ran a hand through his hair as he stood by the table. "Help me understand what's happened."

Roman made a gesture for Leah to talk. She sat on the top of the table and planted her feet on the bench. "Last January I awoke in a ditch about an hour's distance outside of town with no memory of who I was or how I got there."

"Where have you been living?"

She told him of the woman who'd given her food and shelter for the past six months and of how much Colleen had come to mean to her.

"I will be glad to meet this woman and tell her thank you," Clint said.

"You said Sarah was safe, but *how* is she?" Leah asked.

"Coping as best a three-year-old can considering her mother disappeared and someone tried to kidnap her," he replied, and met her gaze.

Guilt and grief that her poor innocent child had become a pawn in this horrible mess grabbed a choke hold on Leah's throat and squeezed. Leah tried not to cry.

"We heard about the incident, but the papers didn't have much coverage," Roman said.

Clint's mouth curved in a wry smile. "Thanks to FBI agent Sam Pierce. He put pressure on reporters to suppress the story."

"Jocelyn's Sam?" Leah asked.

"The same. He's a straight shooter," Clint assured her. "You don't need to be afraid of him when he gets here."

Roman covered Leah's fisted hand with his own. Warmth spread up her arm to encircle her heart.

"Can you give us details about the attempted abduction of Sarah?" Roman asked.

"A few weeks after you disappeared," Clint addressed Leah, "a man lured Sarah away from the teachers at the preschool with a puppy. He tried to snatch her, but thankfully another little girl saw what was going on and started screaming. The man took off, leaving the puppy behind, which we now own. Sarah was shaken up but otherwise fine. Jocelyn has been working with Sarah ever since you left."

"Did they catch the guy?" Roman asked.

"Yes. The FBI did. A man named Finch confessed to the kidnapping attempt. He claims some woman hired him over the phone to take Sarah."

Leah caught the glance Roman gave her. "It wasn't me."

"I know," he said, his expression softening. "But it might have been the person who abducted you."

"Well, actually, the FBI thinks a woman named

Angelina Loring was the one who hired Finch," Clint interjected.

The woman's name rang an alarm inside Leah's head. "I have a vague recollection of arguing with her, but…that's it."

Clint studied her for a moment. "They found her body floating in the swamp outside of town. The theory is Dylan Renault killed her."

"And then someone killed him," Roman stated.

"There's been a lot of unexplained deaths in Loomis of late," Clint said. "The FBI were convinced you were dead, as well."

"I would have been if not for Colleen."

"You have no idea why you left Sarah with me?" Clint asked, his dark eyes intense.

She shook her head. If only she did. "What did I say when I dropped her off?"

"That you had some business to take care of and wouldn't be gone long. You said you were worried Sarah had seen something when Earl killed himself." His tortured gaze touched hers. "I shouldn't have let you go. I should have known something was wrong. I should have asked more questions."

Leah's heart ached at the amount of guilt in his voice. "Don't blame yourself."

"Did Leah say what Sarah had seen?" Roman asked.

"No, but the FBI agents working the case had some theories. With Angelina and Dylan both dead, the truth will forever be silent."

"Unless I can remember," Leah said, and sent up a silent prayer for her memory to return. She needed to know what had happened, even if the truth was that she'd killed her husband and had left her child to protect her.

Clint moved closer and pulled her into his embrace. "I'm so glad to have you back."

It felt awkward to be held by someone she didn't know. She tried not to stiffen but then tears sprang to her eyes and dissolved her defenses. She sagged against her brother and hated that she had no memory of him or of Sarah.

The strong arms holding her made her feel safe. She breathed in the scent of her brother's aftershave, a spicy, masculine smell. An image burst forth. She, as a little girl, was crawling into the lap of a dark-haired man with a mustache. He laughed, a deep baritone sound, as she tickled him under his chin.

She pulled back and stared at her brother. "I remember a man with a mustache. He wore the same aftershave as you."

Clint's face softened. "That would be our father. I wear the same cologne he did."

Happiness gripped her heart. She had a memory of her father. She turned her gaze to Roman. "I remembered my father."

"That's good," Roman commented. "Slowly, things are returning."

"Have you remembered other things?" Clint asked, and searched her face.

Leah wasn't ready to admit the one memory she wished she could put back into the abyss of her mind.

"A few. I remembered being at the Renault Plantation and I remembered a fight with Earl."

Clint touched her cheek. "It will come back to you. We have to trust that God is in control and He'll restore your memory in His time."

"The waiting is hard," she replied, wishing God would hurry up and reveal everything, even though she knew enough about God's character to know His timing was always perfect.

"I can't wait for you to meet Mandy," Clint said, his dark eyes lighting up from within.

"You say that like I haven't met her before."

Clint shook his head. "You haven't. She's the nanny I hired to care for Sarah. And, well…we've become involved."

Happy that he seemed so happy, Leah managed a smile.

"Do you think this Mandy could be involved in Leah's disappearance? Maybe she wanted Sarah as her own?" Roman asked, his eyes hard and full of suspicion.

Leah's smile died.

Clint chuckled. "No, Roman. She came to Loomis months after Leah disappeared and with her own baggage. I trust Mandy implicitly," Clint said. "I couldn't have made it these past months without her."

Reassured, Leah touched her brother's arm. Compassion and regret scored her deeply. "I'm so sorry you had to go through this, and I can't thank you enough for caring for my baby."

"That's what family's for," Clint replied, his expression tender. "I just thank God you're alive."

"Me, too," she said, and gave him a hug as a tear crested on her lashes. "I want so badly to see Sarah."

"No," Roman interjected. "Not a good idea. You wouldn't want to subject her to more trauma."

"But seeing her might jog loose some more memories," Leah insisted, her voice breaking.

"And could place her in more danger. Remember that a killer is still out there," Roman said in a harsh voice.

Leah sucked in a sharp breath of pain and guilt. Everyone close to her had suffered because of her. Roman was right not to put Sarah in danger or add to her trauma. No, Leah didn't deserve to see her daughter. Not yet.

Not until she knew for sure she wasn't a murderer.

EIGHT

"I agree with Roman," Clint stated. "We can't place Sarah in danger."

"I know," Leah said, trying to keep her disappointment from showing. "And I have to believe that's why I left her with you in the first place. To keep her safe."

"She *is* safe and cared for," Clint said.

The concern and compassion in Clint's expression eased some of Leah's pain.

Clint turned to Roman. "How soon until this lawyer of yours gets here?"

"A matter of hours."

"What then?"

Roman shrugged. "Legally? I don't know. But in the meantime, Leah should stay out of sight."

"No," she said. "I want to know the truth. I *have* to find the truth. And the only way to do that is to unlock my memory." She glanced around the park, her gaze snagging on the stately gazebo in the center. "I want to go over there."

Roman's gaze followed her pointed finger. "Why?"

She shook her head. "I don't know." She faced him.

"Remember the other night when I told you I had a flash of memory about that Loring woman? That gazebo was in the memory."

"Okay, then."

Leah put her hand on her brother's arm. "I need you to be with Sarah. People are going to start talking about me, and she shouldn't hear I'm back from a stranger." Tears welled in her eyes, blurring her vision. "Please tell her I love her and that I'm working real hard to get back to her."

Clint covered her hand with his. "Of course. You do what you need to. Just let me know if I can help."

"You are helping by taking care of my daughter."

Clint smiled and leaned in to kiss Leah on the cheek. "Be safe." To Roman, he said, "Keep me in the loop."

"We will," Roman assured him. "And you'll ask around about Chuck?"

"Yes, I'll stop by and talk to Reverend Harmond on the way home."

"Who's Chuck?" Leah asked as Clint walked away.

"The town drunk and hopefully our witness."

"Right." That poor soul who'd seemed so frightened the other night.

With Roman at her side, Leah strode through the park, dodging a Frisbee and circling around a soccer game. Once they reached the gazebo, Roman halted Leah with a staying hand.

At first glance, the lattice-covered structure looked picture perfect in the setting, surrounded by lush lawns, live oak trees and fragrant azaleas blooming in bright clusters, but on closer inspection she could see the paint was peeling and some of the slats were broken.

"Looks like someone's been living in here," Roman stated as he stepped inside.

Leah joined him on the threshold of the round interior. It did indeed look as if someone had been using the gazebo as a sort of barracks. A tattered blanket lay puddled on the bench, debris from several meals lay scattered on the floor and a book lay open, as if the reader would return any second to pick up where he'd left off.

Leah moved closer and realized the book was a Bible, opened to Proverbs. A profound sadness filled her heart. Someone with faith was living like this. Surely the town, the church, had a program to help the homeless.

"How come this place is so decrepit?" she asked as she turned her attention away from the Bible and gazed out at the beauty of the park. From this vantage point, she could see the whole park.

"This was the scene of a murder," Roman responded.

Leah gasped. "Which one?"

"An old one. If I remember the story right, twenty-five years ago a young mother, Mary Sampson, was killed in this very place just days after Amelia Gilmore disappeared. Amelia left behind her young child, Jodie." His gaze met hers. "Jodie Gilmore went to Loomis High. I think she was a year behind you in school."

"The name doesn't sound familiar."

"People were talking about the town being cursed

and such. This is the South, and it's Louisiana—with all the superstitions that come with it." He gave a humorless laugh. "Not good for the town growth. The town officials started their annual Mother's Day Festival and Mother of the Year Pageant to counteract the nastiness of the rumor mill," Roman said as he picked up the blanket for inspection.

"That's awful," Leah said with a shiver. "Loomis sure has had its share of darkness."

"Sure has." Roman dropped the blanket. "I'm thinking this is Chuck's hangout."

"Seems like a pretty good hiding place," Leah commented. But that wasn't why they were there.

Taking a deep breath and slowly exhaling, she tried to calm her mind as Jocelyn had showed her. She closed her eyes and tried to capture the memory she'd had the other day.

In her mind the day had been cold. She and Angelina were both wearing coats, their breath puffing in the frigid air. Angelina's beautiful face was twisted in anger as she spewed hatred at Leah.

Just because Earl's dead doesn't mean I'm going to let you make a play for Dylan. He's mine. And no whore of a woman and her brat of a kid are going to stand in the way of me marrying Dylan, even if your kid is his.

Leah jerked and her eyelids flew open. "Angelina knew that Sarah was Dylan's. She planned to marry him and was warning me not to get in the way."

"Well, someone got in the way," Roman remarked ironically.

"It wasn't me."

When he didn't respond, Leah's shoulders sagged. Who was she kidding? She had no idea if she did or didn't kill Earl and Dylan. Or Angelina, for that matter.

"I'd like to go see Colleen now," she said, and walked out of the gazebo.

Silence reigned as Roman drove them back to the Peel house. As soon as the truck came to a halt, Colleen had the front door opened and was waiting for Leah. Leah sailed into the older woman's arms, finding comfort from the doubts and accusations that seemed to be constantly chasing her.

"Come along, child. You need to rest and regroup," Colleen murmured soothingly.

Rest and regroup. That sounded like a plan. But an hour and a half later, after answering all of Colleen's questions, the lawyer, Clive Gerade, arrived. Mort had driven to the airport to pick him up, and Leah wasn't sure resting and regrouping would be happening anytime soon as the grueling process of updating the tall, stately gentleman lawyer began.

"So what do you think?" Roman asked Clive when Leah was finished filling the lawyer in on the state of the situation. She'd done a good job of retelling the story of her life since awakening in the ditch. Roman was proud of her.

Clive's expression turned thoughtful. "It's good

you've made contact with a mental-health professional. That will go a long way with the jury if this
should ever go to trial, which I hope to avoid. From the
sound of it, any evidence is circumstantial, but I'll
have a better idea once I know exactly what the police
have."

He put his notepad into his briefcase and snapped the
case shut. "I would suggest, Mrs. Farley, you make another appointment with Dr. Pierce as soon as possible.
The quicker you regain your memory, the better."

Leah rose from the kitchen chair. "I'll call Jocelyn
right now."

Roman watched her leave the room. He turned to
Clive. "What about the witness, Chuck?"

Clive stroked his chin with two fingers. "He could
be a help or not. I'll speak with the sheriff about finding the man."

Roman sneered. "Sheriff Reed didn't seem much
interested in finding a witness. He has his mind set on
Leah as the murderer."

Clive's thin lips curved. "We'll see about that. I did
some checking on my way here, and it seems the
mayor is quite fond of Mrs. Farley. I doubt he would
take kindly to the sheriff obstructing her defense."

Roman nodded, relieved and gratified to know he'd
made the right choice in contacting Clive. In Baton
Rouge, Clive was well known for his tenacity in de-
fending his clients. "What can I do to help Leah?"

Clive rose and placed his hand on Roman's shoulder. "You've done what you can. Leave the rest to me."
The older gentleman then pulled on his suit coat. "Can

you take me into town? I would like to speak with Sheriff Reed."

"Sure. Let me see if Leah was able to reach the doctor."

Roman found Leah just hanging up. "Can she see you?"

"Yes. She's available now."

"Good. I'll take you and Clive into town."

"I want to come, too," Colleen stated from where she sat on the couch.

Mort came through the front door. "Where are we going?"

"We're taking the ladies and Clive downtown," Roman answered.

Roman helped Colleen into the back and then moved aside so Leah could slip in next to her. As Leah passed, the fresh scent of the apple shampoo she used teased his senses, momentarily lifting the smell of the bayou that constantly permeated the humid air. Intense longing to hold her jolted through his system.

She was becoming a part of his life in a way he wasn't sure he liked. Thinking of her in any terms beyond the scope of this current situation wouldn't be a good idea. He had a life to get back to, a score to settle. She didn't fit into the equation.

Once everyone was seated, Mort drove them to the main section of Loomis and dropped off Clive at the sheriff's station. Then Mort pulled the truck in front of Dr. Pierce's office. Roman helped the ladies out of the vehicle.

"I'll just go to the bakery. They've got the best pecan pie," Mort said with a grin before driving away.

Roman escorted the women into the waiting room. Colleen sank into a chair while Leah moved to stand near the toy box. Roman's heart squeezed at the sad expression on Leah's face.

"Well, hello, everyone," Doctor Pierce said as she came out of her office.

She was tall, pretty, with dark blond hair and striking blue eyes that regarded Leah with kindness. For that, Roman was grateful.

Leah stepped over to Colleen and laid a hand on the older woman's shoulder. "Jocelyn, this is Colleen."

Jocelyn held on to Colleen's hand. "Leah told me of your kindness to her. I can't thank you enough for taking such good care of my friend."

The older woman's eyes misted. "I've come to love her like a granddaughter."

The doctor nodded and then shifted her attention to Roman.

Her gaze, though kind, had a speculative gleam as she regarded him. "Mr. Black. You've also been very kind, and I thank you. I understand you were friends with Clint in high school."

"Yes, we were," he replied, feeling a bit like a bug under a microscope.

"Did you also know Ava and Dylan Renault? Max Pershing?"

"I knew of them but had no real personal contact with them. We didn't run in the same crowds," Roman responded. Talk about an understatement.

The Renaults and Pershings were the upper crust of Loomis, while he'd barely been the underbelly. Especially after his mother died. He'd been nothing but trouble then. Not someone the esteemed folks of Loomis cared to rub elbows with.

"My husband, Sam, will be here soon. Until then, let's get to work on your memory, shall we, Leah?" Doctor Pierce drew Leah into the inner office and shut the door, leaving Roman and Colleen to wait.

"Is there anything I can get for you while we're in town?" Roman asked the older woman, who now had her nose buried in another magazine.

She lifted her gaze to meet his. "More magazines. I declare, I've become addicted to the tabloid gossip."

"Sounds like you'll fit right in with the Loomis townsfolk," he quipped. "I know Mort got your medicines and all, but would you like another walker?"

She beamed. "Why, young man, you are a dear. That would be lovely. No wonder Leah is so taken with you."

Roman arched his eyebrows. "Taken with me?"

Colleen gave him a look. "Now, don't be coy. You know very well you've come to mean a great deal to that gal. I fair believe she's fallen for you hard."

Roman was glad he was sitting down, because the world just tilted. Fallen for him?

"And why wouldn't she?" Colleen continued. "God brought you to us when we needed you and that says a lot, if you ask me."

"God didn't bring me to you, I found you on my own," he retorted, still trying to sort out how he felt about Colleen's little revelation.

Did Leah have feelings for him? And how did *he* feel about that? He liked her and cared about her well-being, but did his own feelings run deeper? Could he allow them to?

"Bah, *on your own*." Colleen chuckled. "God's in control, young man, not you. He wanted her found and He made it possible. You should be grateful to know God used you to work out His will."

God had used him to work out His will? The thought wrapped around him and covered him with a cloak of comfort. Roman liked that. Liked that thought a lot. From the day he'd decided to invite Christ into his life, Roman had only wanted to follow God and know Him deeply. But it was hard to surrender sometimes, hard to believe that God was really in control. Being used by Him to do good made Roman feel loved.

His cell phone vibrated at his hip. He checked the caller ID and stilled. The call was from his friend within the Baton Rouge police department. Roman sent up a silent prayer that whatever Karl had to report was good news.

"Excuse me," he said to Colleen as he stepped outside to take the call.

"Karl," Roman answered.

"Hey, good buddy." Karl's raspy voice came over the line. "You won't believe what popped up on the NCIC link today."

Roman closed his eyes as hope flared. The National Crime Information Center's computer database made it possible for law enforcement to catch criminals across state lines and jurisdiction. "You got a hit."

"Yeah. I saw something come across my desk a few days ago and decided to run that print you gave me again, and today it came back with a verifiable match. Your man, an Ethan Stumps, is in Hattiesburg, Mississippi. He was picked up on a rape charge, but the charges were rescinded. I have his address."

Roman sagged against the brick building as everything he'd worked toward for the past twenty years was finally within reach. "Text me the information," he managed to say before hanging up.

Finally, he would serve justice on the man who destroyed his mother's life. His prayers had been answered. "Thank You, Lord," he whispered.

He pushed away from the wall. Adrenaline pumped through his veins and plans formulated in his mind as he impatiently waited for Leah to finish her session.

"We made some good progress," Jocelyn said. "The key is to relax and not let the fear of remembering overwhelm you."

"I'll try not to," Leah said. Jocelyn may have thought they'd progressed but Leah hadn't really remembered much that would help solve the murders. She had, however, remembered more of her father. She remembered he'd taught her to ride a bike and he'd helped her with her math when she was a kid. The memories were a soothing balm to her heart.

There was a quick knock on the door before the door opened. A tall man wearing a dark suit and red tie entered. His dark brown hair was cut short and his tanned skin implied a lot of time spent outdoors. His brown eyes assessed Leah before his gaze moved to Jocelyn. His expression softened, making him more handsome.

"Sam!" Jocelyn glided from her chair to hug her husband.

Roman filed in right behind the FBI agent, his expression grim. Leah suppressed a shiver of apprehension. *Don't let the fear overwhelm you,* Jocelyn had just said. That was easier said than done.

Roman came to stand beside Leah as she rose to greet them, also. He gave her an inquiring glance. She shook her head to indicate she hadn't remembered anything useful. He gave a quick nod of acknowledgment before he turned his attention back to the other man. "Agent Pierce has some questions for you."

Sam stepped forward, his hand outstretched. "It's good to finally meet you, Mrs. Farley. Jocelyn has been very worried about you."

Leah accepted his offered hand. His handshake was firm but not crushing. "Nice to meet you, too, I think."

Sam flashed a smile, though his eyes searched her face. "This is just an informal meeting, though I will have to have you come to the station for a formal statement later. Jocelyn has filled me in on your amnesia— and your claim that Dylan Renault raped you."

The way he said "claimed" made Leah's insides quake. "It could be a false memory," she said, hating the word *rape*. It sounded so dirty. Made her feel dirty.

Roman visibly stiffened. "Shelby Mason can confirm that they were drugged during the Renault Christmas party just prior to Leah's pregnancy."

Leah glanced at him and wondered at the hardness in his eyes.

Sam's gaze turned just as hard as Roman's. "Yes, we've heard Miss Mason's statement. Only DNA testing will confirm the ID of Sarah's biological father beyond doubt."

"But if you do that, then everyone will know I was raped, or think that I had an affair with Dylan Renault," Leah said, not liking that scenario at all. "I don't want everyone to know."

Jocelyn reached for Leah's hand. "Honey, hiding the truth is never a good thing."

"The rape will come out if you are tried for Dylan's murder," Sam said.

Leah gasped. "You don't really believe I killed him, do you?"

Roman stepped protectively closer to Leah. "Agent Pierce, someone else is at work here. There have been three attempts made on Leah's life."

Roman's visible show of support meant the world to Leah. Especially since she wasn't sure if he really believed in her innocence.

A thoughtful expression crossed Sam's face. "That does make things more interesting." His intense gaze pinned Leah to the floor. "But who has motive to get rid of you?"

"I don't know. I wish I did," Leah said as tears burned the backs of her eyes. "There's so much locked up inside here." She thumped a knuckle against her temple. Recalling the conversation she and Roman had had after they'd learned she had worked for the mayor, she asked, "Could the attempts on my life be connected to my work at the mayor's office?"

Sam's eyebrows rose. "Intriguing theory. One worth checking into. The mayor has been adamant that you are innocent and has kept a close eye on the investigation into your disappearance. Now I'm wondering if maybe I should look into him and the workings of city hall."

One of Roman's dark eyebrows shot up. "I'm surprised you haven't already."

Jocelyn raised her hands as if to separate two kids about to go for each other's throats. "The authorities have had no reason to suspect Mayor Charbonnet. He's a good man, who loved Leah like a daughter." She turned her gaze to Leah. "Do you have any recollection of your work at the mayor's office?"

Leah grimaced apologetically. "No, but maybe if I go to city hall, I might remember something useful."

"It's worth a try," Sam said. "Shall we?" He made a sweeping gesture with his hand toward the door.

Jocelyn reached for Leah's hand and squeezed it reassuringly. "I'll come, too."

Leah glanced at Roman for his support. He inclined his head toward the door. "It's a good idea."

"You'll come?" Leah asked.

Roman shook his head. "I think it would be better if I take Colleen back to the house."

She didn't want him to leave her. She wanted him at her side always. But that wasn't a realistic expectation. "I'd appreciate that."

In the waiting room, Leah helped Colleen to stand. Roman placed a new walker in front of her.

Leah captured Colleen's hand. "I'm going to go with Agent Pierce and Dr. Pierce to city hall, where I used to work. We're hoping being back there will jog my memory."

"Where you still work. I'm certain no one fired a treasure such as you, my girl," Colleen said.

Leah smiled. "Thank you for your vote of confidence."

Tears glistened in Colleen's eyes. "I never should have kept you like I did. May the good Lord be as quick to forgive me as you have."

Tenderness welled in Leah's heart. "Shh, Grandmother. Of course you're forgiven."

"I'll come to city hall, too," Colleen said gamely.

"You need to take your medicine. Roman will take you back to the house," Leah said. "I won't be long." At least she hoped not.

Roman held Colleen's arm as he escorted her to the truck, where Mort was waiting. Sam opened the back door to a dark green Ford sedan. Leah slipped inside as Jocelyn went around to the front passenger seat and Sam slid into the driver's seat.

When Mort pulled the truck away from the curb and passed the sedan going in the opposite direction, an acute sense of isolation hit Leah in the chest.

Jocelyn turned in her seat and smiled. "It's going to be all right."

Leah could only pray so.

City hall shared a parking lot with the library. The stately two-story brick building had inviting benches around the outside and beautifully landscaped bushes and flowers. Leah followed Jocelyn and Sam up the wide concrete staircase to the thick oak double doors. Inside the echoing foyer, they approached the security gate.

Sam flashed his badge and they were admitted.

The security guard, an older gentleman with kind hazel eyes, regarded Leah in surprise. "Why, Mrs. Farley, y'all are back. We sure have missed seeing your smiling face."

Disconcerted, Leah gave the man a tentative smile. "Thank you... I'm sorry, I don't remember your name."

He stared at her as if she'd lost her mind. Which, ironically, she had.

"Jeb Henry."

"Good to see you then, Jeb," Leah said, and was thankful when Sam took her by the elbow and led her away. Small talk was hard when only one person in the conversation could remember anything.

"The mayor's office is on the second floor," Jocelyn said, indicating the next wide staircase. Unlike the main staircase, this one was built of marble with an ornately carved banister.

By the time they were at the top, Leah could feel the effort of climbing the stairs in her calf muscles. She must have been in better shape if she'd traversed these stairs every day while working for the mayor.

"You okay?" Sam asked.

"Yes," Leah replied.

As they moved away from the stairs toward the mayor's office at the far west end of the hall, Leah noted the framed paintings of Loomis's past mayors.

All men and most from either the Pershing or the Renault family.

"Quite the gallery," Jocelyn commented. "I hadn't realized how political the Pershings and Renaults were. Though, why I'm surprised, I can't say."

"There are a few not connected to either family," Leah said.

"Well, now, I'd have to correct you on that point," a deep, smoothly Southern male voice intoned.

Leah swung around to find herself staring into the lined, tanned face of a silver-haired older man.

"Most every mayor of this town for the past hundred years has had some connection to one or the other of the two families. Myself included. My great-grandmere was a Pershing on my mother's side."

"Mayor," Sam said, and held out his hand.

"Agent Pierce." He nodded to Jocelyn. "Dr. Pierce."

"Mayor, good to see you again," Jocelyn acknowledged with her own nod.

"Security alerted me to your presence." Then the distinguished-looking man turned his kind gaze toward Leah and regarded her with concern. "Dr. Pierce explained that you are suffering from amnesia."

Leah nodded. "That's correct."

"My dear child, I'm so sorry." He gathered her hands in his. "Ruth has been beside herself with worry over you. She will be mighty glad to see you."

"Ruth?" Another friend?

"My wife," the mayor explained.

"Please give her my best," Leah said, feeling the

need to be polite regardless of the fact that she didn't remember her or the mayor.

"Mayor," Sam said, his voice turning authoritative. "I need to ask you a few questions. Was there anything of a sensitive nature going on here in the mayoral office at the time of Leah's disappearance? Have you received any threats? Anything unusual happen at all?"

The mayor thought for a moment. "Not that I recall. Deputy Olsen asked me the same questions back at the time."

Jocelyn put her arm around Leah. "We're hoping that if Leah can be at her place of work she might have a breakthrough in her memory."

"By all means." Mayor Charbonnet gestured toward the office from which he'd come out. "Leah, please take your time."

"Thank you, sir," she replied, and walked into the mayor's office.

At first glance, she didn't remember the opulent, richly appointed space. The large room was sectioned off for two work areas. The larger portion of the room, with a wide mahogany desk, leather captain's chair, set of standing flags and bookcase loaded with official-looking volumes, was obviously the mayor's workspace.

A smaller, though no less expensive-looking desk sat near the window. A computer, filing cabinet and another bookshelf flanked the desk. Behind it, a brunette with tortoiseshell glasses who sported a little bling at the temples sat, typing. Her fingers flew across the keyboard. When the phone rang, she answered with one hand while the other remained actively typing.

As soon as the young woman was off the phone, the mayor said, "Rachel, would you give us a moment, please?"

"Sure thing, Pops." Rachel rose, grabbed her purse and headed toward the door. "Just page me when I can come back."

When Rachel disappeared out the door, the mayor gave them a sheepish grin. "My youngest, home from college." He addressed Leah, "After you disappeared, I hired a succession of temps through All Temps Employment Agency. None were as good as you. So when Rachel came home, I offered her the position. But when you are ready, your job is waiting for you."

His kind words brought tears to Leah's eyes. "Thank you, sir. You have no idea how much that means to me."

Sam steered the mayor out into the hall. "Mayor, let's step out so the ladies can get to work."

Once the men vacated, Jocelyn gestured toward the room at large. "Wander around a bit. Sit in your old chair," Jocelyn instructed. "Relax your mind and breathe. Be open to whatever comes in. You're safe."

Leah nodded, trying to do as instructed. She took deep, calming breaths as she slowly walked around the office and touched the equipment. She sat in the chair behind her old desk. She placed her hands flat on the desktop. She closed her eyes, picturing herself here working, answering phones, typing, filing.

From the deep recesses of her mind a memory rose. She sat at this desk, the phone rang. She could see herself answer.

Her heart rate picked up. Her breathing turned shallow.

"Leah, breathe," Jocelyn said softly.

Forcing air in through the constriction in her throat, she remembered that phone call. Dylan was on the line. Leah's eyes flew open. "Dylan called me. He wanted me to meet him at Renault Hall. He said he wanted to discuss Sarah."

"Good. Anything else?"

She shook her head. "No." She couldn't keep the disappointment from her voice. "I don't think what happened to me has anything to do with the mayor or my work here."

Jocelyn inclined her head. "I tend to agree."

Leah rose and they joined the gentlemen in the hall. Jocelyn explained the new memory.

The mayor seemed relieved. "I'm glad nothing we had going on here had caused you pain."

"Thank you for your time, Mayor," Sam said as he led the way back toward the stairs.

Just as they were descending, the *clickity-clack* of heels on the marble floor drew Leah's attention. A stunning blonde approached from the east wing of the second floor. Her tight, form-fitting black dress with a short jacket looked both professional and stunning.

The woman jerked to a stop when her gaze met Leah's. "I'd heard you'd resurfaced. It takes some nerve to return after what you've done."

Stunned by the attack, Leah could only stare as anger bubbled in her system. This woman definitely didn't ring any bells, but she did push some buttons.

"Coral, mind your manners," Jocelyn said with a good dose of irritation in her voice.

The blonde arched an eyebrow high. "We've all heard she's responsible for Dylan's death, not to mention her own husband's. And to think she abandoned her own child, too. *Tsk, tsk.*"

"I did not kill either of them," Leah said hotly as tears of anger and shame burned her eyes. She hadn't deliberately abandoned her daughter. *She hadn't.*

"That's not what the sheriff thinks."

Coral's smug smile nearly pushed Leah over the edge. She balled her fists, ready to explode. Only Sam, stepping between Jocelyn and Leah, taking each of them by the elbow, gave Leah the sanity to hold her anger in check.

"Ladies, shall we?" Sam said, maneuvering them past the blond busybody.

Once outside, Jocelyn seethed. "That woman. I can't stomach her."

"I'm sure she's stating what everyone in this town thinks," Leah said, her shoulders sagging. "And they'll only think worse of me when they learn Dylan really is Sarah's father."

Jocelyn gathered Leah's hands in her own. "Honey, you did nothing wrong. You were the victim."

"Why doesn't it feel that way?" Leah asked. "Why do I feel dirty and ashamed?"

Jocelyn's voice gentled. "Believe it or not, those are common reactions of rape survivors. Denying the rape happened won't make your pain go away. Only by dealing with it will you be healed." Jocelyn hugged Leah tightly. "We will work through this together."

Leah held on for a moment as she fought her tears. "Thank you."

Jocelyn leaned back with a smile. "You can't live your life afraid of the gossipmongers of Loomis. Besides, Coral has her own baggage to carry around. She falsely accused Shelby's fiancé, Patrick, of rape back in college, but then the truth came to light that she'd lied. I'm sure she's just glad the gossip mill in town is off her and on to you. And soon it will go on to something else. Always does."

Leah appreciated Jocelyn's attempt to make her feel better.

Nothing changed the fact that once the world knew she had been raped, she'd carry the stigma of being victimized for the rest of her life.

There had to be a way to keep the rape secret while the rest of the truth was brought forward. There just had to be.

NINE

"You're what?" Leah asked, sure she hadn't heard Roman correctly. "Leaving? Now?"

His expression begged her to understand, but she didn't. She paced away from him on the small patio outside the back door of the Peel house. A rusty patio set dominated the cement floor and an empty oak barrel sat forlornly at the edge of the patio as if waiting for someone to take notice and plant cheery flowers in its interior. Leah felt anything but cheery.

"I know this seems abrupt, but I have to. You'll be well taken care of here now. Clive has everything handled. Your brother is available if needed, and you've got Colleen to keep you company while you work with Jocelyn."

"But how come? Can't whatever it is wait? What if someone comes after me again?" She really didn't want to go through this without him. He'd become her rock, her anchor through this stormy nightmare.

He pulled her to the metal chairs and sat with her beside him. His expression beseeched her to understand. Taking her hands in his, he said, "I told you my mother died. But that isn't the whole truth. She didn't just die, she killed herself."

Her heart filled with pain. "Oh, Roman, I'm so…sorry. Why? How come she would do such a thing? How could a mother do that?"

"She was driven to it by the torment of—" He swiped a hand over his chin as if trying to gather his composure. "She was raped, Leah."

A spasm of agony tightened in her stomach as tears burned the backs of her eyes. His mother had suffered the same fate she had, only instead of suicide, Leah's memory had vacated, leaving her child abandoned just as Roman's mother had left him. She reached out to hug him, to offer what little solace she could.

He eased her back, his hands firm on her upper arms. "I've waited twenty years to find the man who attacked my mother. Now, my prayers have finally been answered."

His words didn't compute in her brain. "I don't understand. The man wasn't arrested at the time?"

"No. He vanished, leaving my mother broken and abused."

A dreadful feeling stirred low in the pit of her stomach. "Then how do you know who he is?"

He closed his eyes a moment as if the answer were too hurtful to say. When he opened his eyes, there was such hatred and malice in their inky depths that she leaned away from him, not out of fear as much as surprise.

"I saw it happen. I saw him rape my mother. And I couldn't stop him," he uttered.

Horror, stark and vivid, gripped her by the throat. "You said your mother died when you were eighteen."

A muscle ticked in his jaw. "Five years after the rape."

She did the math. And what it added up to sent dismay spiraling through her. "You were, what? Thirteen? You can't blame yourself, Roman. How could you have stopped it?"

His gaze turned to the landscape, but she sensed he wasn't seeing the dry grass or the cypress trees. "I should have been able to. My mother worked as a cocktail waitress for the Blue Oyster Bar. At nights, she'd stash me in the storage room with my comic books and a cot."

He swallowed, his Adam's apple bobbing. "One night, she was closing up and a customer she'd had a problem with earlier in the evening slipped in again through the back door. I heard a noise that was out of place. I went to investigate and saw him forcing himself on her. I grabbed a chair and hit him with it. He backhanded me and sent me flying. But I still saw what he did. Then he was gone, and my mother was on the floor, sobbing. He'd busted her nose, as well as raped her."

A deep, gut-wrenching ache filled Leah's soul. No child should have to witness such violence. She hated that there was so much evil in the world. Evil that had touched both of their lives.

She slid her arm around his shoulders and laid her head against his biceps, offering the only comfort she could. There were no words that would adequately convey the empathy she felt for him and his mother. Were these deep feelings echoes of her past? Had she felt the same way when she'd discovered her dead husband?

"If you knew what he looked like, why didn't the police arrest him?" she asked, her voice shaky with tears of grief.

"Like you said, I was a kid. They didn't listen much to me, nor did they try very hard to find him." The anger in his tone echoed through the stillness of the backyard.

"But your mother's testimony? Surely the authorities listened to her."

"My mom denied it. Said she'd fallen to explain her busted nose. She didn't want anyone to know what had happened. She wanted to keep it a secret."

Her whole being stilled. She understood his mother's desire not to tell. Leah hadn't told when Dylan raped her, and she still didn't want anyone to know. Yet, look how keeping the truth hidden had destroyed Roman's mother. Leah's heart hurt. "So that's why you went into law enforcement? So others wouldn't have to go through the same thing?"

He gave a short, brittle laugh. "No, my reasons weren't that honorable. I became a cop to track down the dirtbag. I'd saved a shot glass the man drank from, and as soon as I was on the force, I started running his prints. Today there was finally a hit. He raped again."

Her mouth dried out. She was almost afraid to ask—knowing he was capable of killing someone in cold blood would be hard to deal with. But her need to know outweighed her need to sugarcoat the situation. "You want revenge."

"I want justice," he said, his voice hard-edged. He stood and paced.

"What will that give you?"

He glanced at her. "Peace. Satisfaction. Redemption. Take your pick."

Everything inside her shrank from him now. Her deep faith made her sadly aware of how mistaken he was. "You won't find any of those. Vengeance isn't yours to take."

The muscle in his jaw twitched. "I know. I know. 'Vengeance is mine, sayeth the Lord.' I've heard the scripture. But that doesn't mean the guy should be allowed to get away with what he did." His hands fisted at his sides. A hard light entered his gaze. "He has to pay."

Her breath seized in her lungs, making her chest tight. With effort, she said, "You want to kill him."

"Yes. I want to extract the justice due my mother."

"But you can't. Only God can claim justice," she cried.

"God brought me this opportunity," Roman argued, his jaw set in a stubborn line.

"God wouldn't orchestrate a murder. Ever. And that's what you're talking about. Murdering this man as an act of revenge. You'll lose your soul if you make that choice."

"The man has to pay," he insisted, his dark eyes flashing with rage.

"But you can't be his judge, jury and executioner. How can you think that in choosing to do this you'll gain any peace?"

He spun away from her, his hands flexing at his sides. "I have to go, Leah."

She rose from the chair, her hand outstretched. If she could physically touch him, she might be able to reach his heart and soul. "No, Roman, you don't *have* to. You *choose* to. Please don't choose to be like him."

The back door banged open as Mort came bounding out. "Hey, I…" He stopped in his tracks, his gaze going from Leah to Roman. "Am I interrupting something?"

"No," Roman said, his face a mask of stone. "What do you want?"

Mort blinked. "Uh, Deputy Olsen called. Chuck's been spotted at the old Renault estate. Olsen said he'd give us first crack at talking to him before he passed on the information to the sheriff." A gleam entered Mort's hazel eyes. "I think Deputy Olsen's looking to replace the sheriff, if you ask me."

"He'd be good for this town," Roman replied, his gaze never leaving Leah's face. "Let's go find Chuck and get him to talk."

Leah nearly crumbled in relief. He wasn't leaving, at least not yet. As she followed the men to the truck, she sent up a silent plea to the Lord for guidance. How could she make Roman understand that two acts of evil would only result in more pain?

Roman stole a glance at Leah. She sat between him and Mort in the cab of the truck as they rambled through Loomis toward the Renault plantation house. The pensive expression on her lovely face made him wonder if she were thinking about his revelations.

Why he'd told Leah of his mother's rape was beyond him. He never talked about that night to anyone.

He'd had girlfriends in the past, but he'd never felt compelled to share his private grief with any of them the way he had felt compelled to do with Leah.

Maybe it was her current situation that made him feel the need to open up. Or maybe the things Colleen had said about Leah being taken with him had softened his heart and turned his brain to mush.

Roman just didn't know what to think or feel. His heart told him to listen to Leah, but his mind screamed that he had to take the opportunity presented or he'd never redeem himself, never be able to live fully.

The need for revenge and his faith warred inside his mind, heart and soul, causing a riot of acid to churn inside him. Where were the antacids when you needed them?

He forced himself to focus on finishing what he'd started here in Loomis—protecting Leah and making sure that justice was served in her case, to whatever end that led.

Once they found Chuck and discovered whom he'd seen, Roman would then be able to leave without feeling as if he'd failed Leah. At least he hoped.

Mort brought the truck to a halt near the dilapidated front gate. "This place gives me the creeps," he stated.

"Me, too," Leah agreed.

Roman opened the door, anxious to get this done. "Mort, you circle around the left side of the house, and Leah and I will go around the right side. If you find Chuck, detain him," Roman instructed before stepping out of the truck.

He turned to help Leah out of the cab. She offered him a smile as she took his offered hand. Her delicate fingers closed around his and the pressure she exerted sent tingles zinging up his arm to curl through his chest and wrap around his heart.

He tried to fight the welling of affection coming up from his very depths. The desire to be who she wanted him to be blasted through him like a rocket launcher. But he couldn't be that person. Not until he had justice for his mother.

Releasing Leah's hand, he stepped away, as if distance between them would alleviate some of his inner turmoil. She gave him a curious look before grabbing the Thermos of black coffee they'd brought just in case they would need to sober Chuck up.

He held the gate open for her to pass through, then followed her through the overgrown front garden. The scent of summer flowers mingled with the decaying smell of plant life gave the hot Louisiana air a putrid tinge. They rounded the corner of the house and stopped beside the looming stone birdbath with the huge brass pelican clutching the side.

Leah stared at the fountain, lines of concentration marring the delicate skin around her eyes and mouth. Then she shook her head. "I hate this ugly thing."

"Do you remember anything else?" Roman asked.

"No, nothing new. Just that flash of red." She looked around. "Do you think Chuck is inside the main house? Or could he be in there?" she asked, pointing toward the garage.

Mort came to join them and gestured toward the house. "I'll look inside if you two want to take the garage."

"That works," Roman said.

Leading Leah to the garage, Roman made his way carefully to the side window. The glass was too dirty to see through. They circled around the small building and found a door in the back. When Roman tried the knob, it easily turned in his hand. The hinges squeaked as he pushed the door open and stepped inside. Stale air and another pungent odor met them.

"Phew," Leah said, waving the air away from her nose.

"Alcohol," Roman whispered, and put a finger to his lips. "I think we've found Chuck's other lair."

Dirt covered the cement floor, the wooden wall was in need of repair and the windows were so dingy they muted the sun's glow. In the far corner on top of a pile of burlap sacks and worn blankets, a man lay curled in the fetal position. Short red hair stuck up in all directions from his round head. His face, even in repose, looked haggard with stubble covering his jaw and chin. The clothes hanging on his thin frame had seen too many days and appeared to barely be holding together by the threads.

Empathy blew through Roman, making him wince. How did a man get in this state? He'd never understood homelessness. Was it a product of self-pity or circumstances?

There were places that would provide shelter and food, even in a town like Loomis, yet here Chuck was, reeking of alcohol and living in an abandoned building.

Shaking off his unproductive thoughts, Roman shook Chuck awake.

"Whaaat?" Chuck muttered, and batted at Roman's hands.

"Wake up," Roman said. "We need to talk to you."

Chuck grumbled and groused as he sat up, holding his head as if to keep it on. "Ugh. Why'd ya go 'n wake me? I was haven' a good dream."

Roman squatted down to eye level with the man and ignored the stench emanating from his foul breath. "Chuck, listen. We need your help."

Chuck frowned and wiped the back of his hand across his mouth. "I can't help no one."

Leah moved forward with the Thermos. "Here, drink this."

The smell of coffee chased the less favorable odors away. Chuck eyed Leah and the coffee suspiciously. "How do I know you ain't gonna poison me with that?"

"Why would we want to poison you?" Leah asked.

"You work for her, don't you?"

"Who?" Roman asked.

Chuck shook his head, agitation making his movements jerky. He cringed from Roman. "I told her I wouldn't say nothing."

Anticipation mounted. Roman tried for calm even though he wanted to reach out and shake the answers out of the man. But first he had to sober him up. "Look, I'll drink some first." He drank from the Thermos. "See, no poison."

With a shaky hand, Chuck reached out and drank from the Thermos. Roman exchanged a glance with Leah. The guy was a little nutty.

"Tell us about the red-haired woman," Leah said in a soothing tone.

Chuck recoiled. "No."

"You saw her hurt someone," Roman prompted, trying to keep his voice even.

Chuck scrambled away until he was wedged in the corner, his hands covering his ears. "No, no, no. I won't tell."

Frustration gripped Roman in a tight vice. He stood and clenched his jaw as he stared at the cowering man. "This is getting us nowhere."

Leah put her hand on his arm, the pressure enough to grab his attention. "Let me try."

Roman made a "go ahead" gesture with his hand.

She moved to where Chuck rocked on his heels. Lowering herself to a sitting position, she said, "Chuck, no one is going to hurt you. We won't let them. But we really need you to tell us what you saw."

Chuck shook his head.

"Do you know who I am?" she asked.

His head bobbed up and down.

"The police say I killed my husband and Dylan Renault."

Chuck's eyes widened. He shook his head vigorously. "You didn't kill no one."

Hope that he could help clear her name made her voice shaky. "No, Chuck, I didn't. At least I don't think so. You see, I can't remember. Someone hit me on the head and I've lost my memory." She tried to appeal to his conscience. "I need you to help me."

Chuck's face screwed up tight. "*She* hit you!"

Heart beating wildly, Leah said, "She did?"

He nodded as he moved closer. "Who else would?

You're lucky she didn't use her gun on you the way she did the others. She's a coward."

Ignoring his stench, Leah laid her hand on his arm. "Who did you see her shoot?"

He seemed to shrink. His gaze darted around as if he was worried someone would overhear. "Earl. Dylan. Angelina."

Leah's gaze flew to Roman. He made a rolling motion with his hand, which she figured meant keep Chuck talking. She focused back on the man beside her. "Please tell me who killed them. Who hurt me?"

He clutched her hand. His bloodshot eyes implored her. "You sure you won't let her hurt me?"

"I promise."

He shook his head and backed away. "You won't believe me. She said no one would believe me."

Holding on to her patience by a thin thread, Leah said, "I promise I'll believe you."

For a moment his blurry-eyed gaze searched her face as if trying to decide if she was telling the truth. He clamped his jaw tight and shook his head.

"You saw her face?" Leah probed. She needed him to tell her who he saw. "Please, tell me. Does she have red hair?"

"A red wig." He wrinkled his nose. "And she stinks."

"Stinks?"

"Yeah. A sickly sweet kinda stink."

Leah sat back on her heels. She'd remembered a sickly sweet smell when she'd recalled the bird fountain. "Did you see this woman here, at the fountain?"

"Maybe," Chuck said, stubbornness tightening the

lines around his mouth. "I'm not gonna say any more. I don't want to be knocked on the head and shot in the back and left for dead."

"The police could protect you," Leah said, hoping to convince him to cooperate. "You could enter the witness protection program. Have a second chance at life."

"I don't want to leave Loomis. It's my home," he said, growing more agitated. "You best just leave me be. I ain't gonna tell you anything."

Frustration needled at Leah as she stood and joined Roman by the door. Disappointment pushed at her shoulders. "You're right, this was a waste of time. He refuses to say anything else even though he knows who the killer is."

"We could take him to the sheriff or the FBI."

"That seems to be the only option. Maybe they'd have better luck getting him to reveal who the woman with the red wig is," Leah said.

"Or I could beat it out of him," Roman said darkly.

She gave him a droll stare, not sure if he was serious. "No."

Mort opened the door. "Hey, you two. Any luck?"

They quickly filled him in.

"Bummer. Thought for sure we'd get a break," Mort said. "Now what?"

"I need you to help me get Chuck into the truck," Roman said. "We'll take him to the sheriff's station and then we'll go back to the house. Maybe Clive will have had a more productive day."

They moved back to where Chuck had curled into a ball. Leah bent down and tugged on his arm. "Come with us."

He shied away from her. "Where?"

"We're going to get you some food." Roman helped Chuck to his feet.

Reluctantly, he allowed Roman to lead him outside, where they piled back into the truck, with Mort driving. They drove away from the old plantation house, toward town. The stench of alcohol filled the cab. Leah rolled down her window.

"Is that the Renaults' home?" Roman asked, gesturing to the stately house coming into view.

Chuck whimpered and hunkered down in the seat. "Don't let her see me."

Leah frowned at Chuck's reaction. Could the "she" he'd referred to be someone in that house?

"Yep, that's the Renault's," Mort replied as he slowed the truck. "The story goes Charla Renault had this newer house built within view of the old plantation house so she could watch the place rot from her bedroom window."

"How come she would do that?" Leah asked. "Hasn't the plantation house been in the family for a long time?"

Mort shrugged. "According to Harvey at the barber shop, Mrs. Renault hated her father, so when she inherited the house, she vowed never to live there again."

"Something bad must have happened to her there for her to have that much hate," Leah said. "It's sad."

"That's a little nuts, if you ask me," Roman said.

Leah thought about that for a moment. Her gaze

strayed to Chuck, cowering as far down on the seat as possible. Something or someone in that house had the poor man scared to death. "Stop the truck."

"Why?" Roman asked.

Gesturing to Chuck, Leah said in a low voice, "Someone in that house may be the 'she' he was talking about."

He considered her for a moment. "Maybe. But you know Mrs. Renault could have the sheriff arrest us for harassment or stalking."

"Maybe, but wouldn't that cause more of a scandal? Besides, all she has to do is refuse to see us, but I think we should try to talk to her." Motioning to Chuck, Leah said, "He's obviously scared just seeing the Renault home."

"Maybe that's because he belongs in the loony bin," Roman muttered.

Leah touched Roman's hand. "I'd like to at least go see the woman. See if someone in that house is a murderer. Or at the very least find out if Mrs. Renault knew about the blackmail."

He curled his fingers around hers, sending ripples of affection sliding through her.

"I think it's a waste of time," Roman stated.

"But it's all we have at the moment," she reminded him gently.

"Fine."

She smiled with gratitude and a bit of pleasure that he agreed. Working together as a team was a gratifying experience. She could only hope he'd see how well they worked together and not take off to… She didn't even want to think about what Roman wanted to do.

Mort brought the truck to a halt at the curb. "Do I have to come? Mrs. Renault scares me," Mort said, his thin face showing his distaste.

Roman chuckled. "No, you go on and take Chuck to the sheriff's station. I'll give you a call when we're ready to be picked up."

Leah followed Roman out of the truck. As Mort pulled away from the curb, Chuck's face pressed against the back window. His worried eyes sent slivers of apprehension cascading down Leah's spine.

They might be confronting a murderer.

TEN

Leah gave herself a shake. She shouldn't let Chuck's psychosis make her wary. She had a mystery to solve. And someone in this house might provide the answers to the questions plaguing her. Determinedly, she led the way to the large, ornately carved front door.

She rang the doorbell. The muted echo of a gong rang throughout the house.

A few moments later the door was opened by an older woman in a maid's uniform. She eyed them with suspicion. "May I help you?"

"We'd like to speak with Mrs. Renault," Leah said, glad her voice didn't waver. Now wasn't the time to go weak in the knees.

"Whom shall I say is calling?"

Roman stepped forward and handed the woman a business card.

She nodded and stepped aside so they could enter. The foyer was darkly paneled. A wide staircase with a gleaming banister led upstairs. A round table positioned to catch the sun streaming in through a high window sported a large crystal vase with a huge bouquet of exotic flowers.

"I'll have you wait in the library," the maid said, and led them through a set of double doors and then shut the door behind her as she retreated.

"So what's your plan?" Roman asked.

That was a fair-enough question. She shrugged. "I haven't come up with one yet."

"You know the second she sees you, she's gonna throw us out."

Leah moved to a massive floor-to-ceiling bookcase, marveling at the sheer quantity of books. Some seemed to be very old, the bindings ornate with gold lettering in pounded leather. "Do you think she knows that Sarah is her grandchild?" She cringed even asking the question.

Roman paced to the window overlooking the landscaped backyard. "The way gossip flows in this town, I've no doubt she's heard it. But believe it? Doubtful."

Rumors and innuendo. That's all that was flying around now. But once the truth came out? She hated that people would know she'd been raped. But hiding the rape had only served to cause more problems in the long run. Problems they were all dealing with now. She thought about how Roman's mother had denied being raped, and it had eaten away at her until she'd killed herself. Leah didn't want to suffer the same fate. Not anymore.

Leah turned away from the books to regard Roman. He was a good man despite the trauma he'd suffered. The light coming through the window bathed him in a soft glow, making the starkness of his black clothing seem almost otherworldly. His dark hair gleamed in the sun. She wondered if his hair was silky to the touch or would the texture be coarser? Her fingers flexed, itching to find out. "Should I tell Mrs. Renault the truth of what happened?"

"She'd take that news well," he remarked dryly.

"Right." How did you tell a woman her son was a rapist? Especially when that son had been murdered and thus was unable to defend himself against the charge.

The double doors opened. The whirl of the electric wheelchair announced Mrs. Renault's arrival. The sweet smell of perfume lavishly applied filled the library as she entered with her butler hovering near her side. The scent was vaguely familiar. On Mrs. Renault's lap, a white Jack Russell terrier sat with his front paws on the arm of the wheelchair while his back legs rested on Mrs. Renault's knee.

Hatred twisted in Charla Renault's lined face. "You have some nerve coming to my home."

Leah swallowed back trepidation and stepped forward. "We're sorry to bother you, but we have some questions."

Her gaze narrowed. "Questions? What right have you to question me?" She pointed one narrow finger at Leah. "My son is dead because of you."

"I didn't kill him." Leah moved closer, feeling foolish for having decided to come here. "I have an alibi."

"Bah. Bosworth, call the sheriff," Mrs. Renault cried.

"Dylan wasn't the saint you think he was," Roman

said as he came to stand beside Leah. He placed his hand on the small of her back.

Grateful for his support, she said, "I think my husband may have been blackmailing your son."

"Blackmail!" Mrs. Renault sputtered, growing very agitated. The dog gave a bark and jumped from the wheelchair to scurry out of the library.

Mrs. Renault's complexion molted with red splotches and her eyes grew wide. "Dylan would have told me if anyone was doing something so vile. No one had any reason to blackmail my son. He didn't do anything to be blackmailed for. How dare you besmirch his good name after what you've done?"

"There now, Ms. Charla, don't upset yourself," Bosworth cooed while patting her shoulder in a gesture meant to soothe.

She pushed his hand away. "Get these people out of my house. Have them arrested." She pressed a lever on the wheelchair and spun around, nearly taking Bosworth out at the knees. "Out of my way."

Bosworth followed his mistress but paused at the door. His clear gray eyes regarded them coldly. "You need to leave now."

When they were alone, Leah sighed and sagged back against Roman's shoulder. "That went well."

Roman snorted. "What did you expect?"

"I don't know." She allowed him to lead her toward the front door. "I think if we could search Dylan's room, we'd find something useful."

"I'm sure the police have combed through Dylan's things already. Besides, I thought we were here to see if Mrs. Renault was harboring a killer," Roman replied in a hushed voice.

She sighed. "True. But maybe if—"

From a side room, the maid reappeared to open the front door.

Leah had a spark of brilliance, or at least insanity. "Excuse me, could I use the restroom?"

The maid hesitated for a moment; indecision warred in her eyes.

Leah gave a pained look. "I really gotta go."

Disapproval flashed in the woman's eyes. "I suppose." She shut the front door and gestured toward a door down the hall. "But be quick about it. If Mrs. Renault finds out, she'll be angry with me. She's not nice when she's angry."

"I'll only be a moment," Leah promised. She gestured with her head to Roman, hoping he'd take the hint and distract the maid.

He frowned at her before a dawning light appeared in his black eyes. He gestured toward the library. "I think I left something in there."

"Oh, good grief," the maid huffed, and stalked toward the library.

Leah waited until they disappeared into the library before slipping up the staircase in search of Dylan's room. Maybe she'd find some answers among his things.

The sound of a tinkling bell filled the air. Leah flattened herself against the wall. From below she heard the maid's panicked voice. "Hurry now. I've got to go. Let yourselves out."

Her footfalls echoed as she scurried away.

Leah leaned over the banister railing. Roman arched an eyebrow at her. She gestured with her hand for him to join her. He rolled his eyes, clearly exasperated with her before vaulting silently up the stairs. Impressed by his prowess, she grinned before she darted down the hall. Aware of Roman at her back, she opened a door on her right and peered inside to find a suite with a very masculine motif of navy-and-brown bedding, a dark wood desk and bed and dresser set. Trophies lined the bookcase. Degrees hung on the wall.

Clearly, they'd found Dylan's room. They slipped inside.

"What are you looking for?" Roman asked as she moved to the desk and began thumbing through the papers.

"I don't know." She found plans for renovations of Renault Hall. She showed them to Roman.

"Interesting. Dylan had wanted to turn the old plantation house back into a livable home. Why?" Roman asked.

A horrible thought struck Leah. "Maybe Earl had tried to blackmail him with the knowledge that Sarah really was his child. And…and Dylan was planning to take Sarah from me."

"That's a huge jump," Roman said. "If that were true, someone would have known. I think it's more plausible that Dylan saw an opportunity to make money on the old place."

"Maybe." But she wasn't convinced. "Earl was

going to blackmail Dylan, then Earl ends up dead. Coincidence?" She shook her head. "Maybe Dylan killed Earl and knocked me out to get Sarah."

"But then who killed Dylan?" Roman countered as he lounged against the door, feet crossed and arms akimbo. "And let's not forget Angelina."

Frustrated by the tangled web of mystery surrounding the deaths, she yanked open the drawers of the desk and rummaged through the content? Not finding anything worth noting, she moved to the dresser. "You could help."

"If I knew what I was looking for, maybe I would," he stated.

"Proof that Earl was blackmailing Dylan."

"Right. Like the police wouldn't have found any proof already if it were in here."

She hated that he was right. "Okay." She headed toward him. "Let's check the other rooms."

"For what?"

"I think all of these deaths have something to do with this family. It's the only thing that connects them. Earl may or may not have blackmailed Dylan, but we do know he planned to. Angelina wanted to marry Dylan. I had Dylan's baby. It all comes down to Dylan."

"And Dylan's dead."

Outside, the sound of a car coming up the drive drew them to the window. A foreign-made red sports car parked near the front steps. A pretty blonde climbed out of the vehicle and disappeared out of view.

"Who benefited from Dylan's death?" she asked.

A gleam entered Roman's gaze. "His sister, Ava?"

"His sister, Ava, who drives a red sports car. Maybe Chuck saw Ava Renault. Maybe she's the killer."

"With a penchant for red wigs."

"Exactly." Leah put her hand on the doorknob. "Let's find Ava's suite."

"What if she comes upstairs?"

She shrugged. "We hide?"

He gave her a censuring stare and took possession of her hand. "Let me go first."

His protectiveness pleased her. "After you."

Roman opened the door, stuck his head out and then motioned for Leah to follow him. The sound of someone coming up the stairs threw Leah's heart into overdrive. She'd thought for sure they'd make it to Ava's suite undetected.

"In here," Roman said as he opened the door of the nearest room and pushed her inside.

She gasped when the door shut. The room was dark except for the faint outline from the shade over the window. The overwhelming scent of gardenias brought water to her eyes. She realized the odor was the same one from her nightmares. And from the perfume Mrs. Renault wore.

Leah groped along the wall to find the light switch. She blinked as the overhead fixture filled the room with a bright glow. Roman had his ear pressed against the door. He held up a finger to his lips.

The room was some sort of storage room. Stacks of boxes dotted the floor. An old steamer trunk sat beneath the window. A vanity sat at an angle, the top covered with perfume bottles. And mostly hidden by more boxes was an old-fashioned dressmaker's model with a long-haired red wig perched on top.

Leah's heart galloped in her chest. She backed up a step and clutched Roman's shirt. "Look," she whispered.

"Bingo," he replied.

"We've got to call the police."

He nodded and opened his phone. The grimace on his face didn't bode well. "No bars."

Great. They were trapped without contact to the outside world. "We should take the wig," she said, picking her way through the boxes, searching for something in which to carry the wig out.

Roman found a beat-up garment bag and stuffed the wig inside. Then he rolled it up and tucked the roll beneath his arm. "Let's get out of here."

Leah paused to pick up a pink glass bottle of perfume. One whiff confirmed it contained the liquid that gave off the sickly sweet smell permeating the air. Had Ava used her mother's perfume to confuse anyone should they question the scent?

Roman switched off the light and slowly cracked the door to peer into the hall. Leah's pulse pounded so hard in her veins she thought for sure she'd have an aneurysm any second. Finally, Roman pulled the door wider and they stepped into the empty hall.

Creeping toward the stairs with Roman in the lead, Leah couldn't believe they'd found the wig. They knew who the culprit was. Ava Renault.

From behind her, the whirring sound of Charla Renault's wheelchair froze Leah's blood. She whipped her gaze back just as Charla Renault screamed.

Roman's heart thumped against his ribs as adrenaline kicked in high gear. He spun around, using his free arm to sweep Leah behind him as he faced the dragon in the wheelchair.

"What are you doing here?" Charla demanded.

Forcing Leah back toward the stairs, he said, "We…uh, found what we were looking for."

"Bosworth!" Charla bellowed.

The door to his left opened and Ava Renault walked out of her suite. Her honey-blond hair was swept back and her almond-shaped, green eyes were wide with surprise. "What's going on?"

Leah tugged at Roman's shirt, urging him to keep moving.

Ava moved closer, her gaze riveted on Leah. "Leah? Oh, my word, we thought you were dead."

Leah moved out from behind Roman. "You hoped so, didn't you?"

Roman tried to restrain her and force her behind his back, but she refused.

Confusion entered Ava's gaze. "What? Of course not. Where have you been?"

"I survived your attempt to kill me," Leah spat out.

"You're not making any sense," Ava said, her gaze darting between Leah and Roman. "Don't I know you?" she asked Roman.

Roman didn't answer. Now was not the time to remind her of their separate social classes.

"BOSWORTH!" Charla screeched again.

"Move," Roman urged Leah, fully expecting Bosworth to come running with a gun in hand.

"We found the wig, Ava," Leah said, staying in place. "And this." She held up the bottle of perfume. "You had it on the day you knocked me over the head and dumped me alongside the road."

Perplexity showed on Ava's face. "I have no idea what you're talking about. And that isn't my perfume, it's..." Her green eyes widened. "You two need to leave."

The sound of running feet echoed down the hall. Roman pulled Leah back and shoved the rolled garment bag containing the wig into her arms. He readied himself to meet Bosworth.

The older man skidded to a halt on the top step. His hands were thankfully empty. "What are you still doing here?"

"We're leaving," Roman said, and pushed Leah toward the stairs.

"No one is going anywhere." Charla Renault's voice, low and hard, stopped them.

Roman turned to stare at the gun the Renault matriarch held in her hand. A warning signal clanged in his brain. They were in danger from a gun-toting, wheelchair-bound old woman.

"Mother?" Ava cried as horror spread across her face. Leah gasped.

"Now you've done it," Bosworth muttered.

"Ava, go back to your room," Charla commanded as the chair whirred forward.

"Mother, put that away before you hurt someone," Ava said in a tight, shaky voice.

"You stupid girl," Charla said, shifting the gun in

her daughter's direction and rising from her wheelchair. She walked toward Ava. "Always in the way."

A stunned silence filled the hallway.

Roman couldn't believe it. Charla Renault could walk! And apparently was their murderer.

Ava swayed as if she might keel over. "You can walk."

"Of course, I can walk. But I must admit I enjoy the attention the chair brings," Charla said as she stopped a few feet from Ava. "You should have listened to your mother and gone to your room. There's no help for it now."

Bosworth stepped between Ava and the gun. He held his hands up in entreaty. "Now, Miz Charla, you don't want to go hurtin' Ava. She's all you have left."

"Don't make me use this on you, too," Charla said to Bosworth.

Leah pushed past Roman. "You killed your own son. How could you?"

Charla shifted the gun in Leah's direction. Roman's heart jumped into his throat. He tried to contain Leah, to pull her back behind him to safety, but again she refused. She stalked closer to Charla, seemingly unconcerned by the gun pointed at her chest. "How come you tried to kill me? What did I do to you?"

Roman edged toward Charla, gauging the distance between them so he could tackle her before she shot Leah.

"Dylan wanted that brat of yours. He would've besmirched the Renault name. I couldn't allow that."

Leah's eyes grew round. "You know that Sarah is his child?"

"Why else would he have wanted to seek custody of her?" Charla gestured with the gun. "You seduced him. Made him want his child."

"He raped me!" Leah cried.

Roman gaped at Leah. She'd admitted it publicly. Good for her. If only they weren't staring death in the face, he'd hug her.

Ava gasped, drawing the older woman's attention.

Roman lunged toward Charla. Deftly, she side-stepped him and aimed the gun at his head. "Oh, no, you don't. I knew when you came back to town you'd be trouble." She swore. "If only that idiot Bosworth had done his job and gotten rid of you both, none of this would be happening now."

Eyeing her finger on the trigger, Roman said, "So you had Bosworth try to kill Leah and me before we could return to Loomis. And he used Ava's car."

"Fat lot of good it did," Charla said, her face twisting with malice as she stared at Leah. "I should've killed you when I had the chance. A temporary moment of weakness that won't happen again."

Ava stepped out from behind Bosworth. Tears streaked down her pale face. "Mother, I don't understand." Ava gazed beseechingly at Bosworth. "Why is she doing this?"

"This isn't your mother right now. She's a little out of sorts," Bosworth said, his voice resigned and regretful.

Out of sorts? Roman gaped. The woman was outright crazy.

"Enough chatter." Charla's gaze darted between the

four of them as the gun roamed from one to another like some sick game of Russian roulette.

Roman wasn't about to wait to see if she was going to make good on her threat to kill any of them. He shifted his weight, preparing to launch himself again at the older woman when the doorbell rang.

It was enough of a distraction. Roman pounced on Charla, knocking her sideways into the wall. The loud retort of the gun firing rang in his ears.

Leah screamed as the echo from the gun bounced off the walls. Her gaze collided with Ava's and then they both turned to see Bosworth slump forward onto the floor. Bright red blood spread on the hall carpet. Ava shrieked.

Roman quickly disarmed Charla, sticking the gun in his waistband while easily fending off Charla's attempts to beat her way free.

Feet pounded up the stairs. A man burst into the hall, his expression panicked. "Ava?"

She fell into his arms sobbing. "Oh, Max."

"Someone call 911," Leah said as she checked Bosworth's pulse. "He's still alive."

Max gave her a curious glance as he and Ava disappeared back into her suite. Leah went to Roman. "You okay?"

He nodded and dodged Charla's fist. "You?"

"Good." Leah had so many questions that only Charla could answer. "How come, Mrs. Renault? How come you killed Dylan? And Earl and Angelina?"

Leah's questions only seemed to aggravate the woman more. "They deserved it! They wanted to ruin me. They wanted to ruin the Renaults!" She kicked, her arms flailing with useless blows to Roman's arms while she screamed obscenities.

Shocked by the level of the woman's insanity, Leah stepped out of the way as Ava and Max reappeared from her suite. Max stepped forward to help restrain Charla, which only served to make her even more angry.

"Let go of me! Don't let a Pershing touch me!" Charla screeched.

The sounds of sirens hurtling closer brought hope of some order to the chaos. Leah ran downstairs and out the front door to meet the deputies and the ambulance pulling up outside.

"What's all the commotion, young lady?" Sheriff Reed said as he hitched up his pants over his paunch. "Why are you bothering Mrs. Renault?"

"Oh, come on," Leah said with exasperation. "There's a man dying inside."

She led the way back inside and up the stairs. The paramedics knelt beside Bosworth. "He's lost a lot of blood. We've got to get him to the hospital."

The sheriff seemed mystified by the situation as he gawked at Charla. "Mrs. Renault?"

Clearly having assessed the situation, Deputy Olsen pushed the sheriff aside and assumed control. "Clayton, Jefferies, cuff Mrs. Renault and take her to the station."

The other two deputies jumped to do Olsen's bidding, relieving Roman and Max of the Renault matriarch. They led her out of the house with her hands cuffed behind her back and curses flying from her mouth.

Feeling the need to apologize to Ava, Leah moved

to where Ava and Max stood watching Mrs. Renault being loaded into the back of the sheriff's patrol car. Ava let out a sob as the cruiser pulled away from the curb. Max comforted her with soothing words.

Leah touched Ava's arm. "I'm sorry I accused you of…well, of murder. It never occurred to me it could be your mother."

"What made you suspect me?" Ava asked as she wiped at the tears in her green eyes. Eyes so like Sarah's.

Roman stepped to Leah's side, his arm wrapping around her waist. She leaned against him, taking comfort in his presence.

"There was an eyewitness to the murders. He was really scared of someone in this house. We assumed it had to be you," Roman said.

Ava and Max exchanged a glance.

"Was your witness Chuck Peters?" Max asked.

"How did you know?" Leah asked.

Ava sniffed. "Chuck Peters was the one who called in my brother's murder."

Roman stiffened. "The sheriff didn't say anything about that and it wasn't in the police reports."

"That's because Sheriff Reed is incompetent," Max said with a good dose of antagonism lacing his voice.

"Did Dylan really rape you?" Ava asked, her voice shaky.

Roman's arm tightened around Leah's waist, bolstering her courage. She nodded. "At the company Christmas party four years ago."

Fresh tears spilled from Ava's lashes. "I'm so sorry. For everything my family has done to you."

Touched that Ava would apologize for something not of her doing, Leah said, "You weren't party to any of it. Besides, you're my daughter's aunt. I hope you and I will be friends."

Ava smiled. "I'd like that." Ava sighed. "I'd best call our family lawyer, Mr. Fayard, for Mother."

Max shook Roman's hand before he accompanied Ava back inside the Renault home.

A buoyant sense of weightlessness hit her, making Leah's limbs weak and her head fuzzy. She wasn't a murderer. She was liberated from the oppressive guilt that had hung around her shoulders for so many months. Though she didn't have her memory back, she was free to start over. To love. And she did love. She loved Roman.

She turned in his arms and drew his lips to hers, putting all the love bubbling in her heart into the kiss.

"Hmm," he murmured as they broke apart. "What was that for?"

"For everything. For your belief in me. For pursuing the truth. For making me realize that keeping the past a secret doesn't help. It only hurts more." She grinned. "For just being you. I love you, Roman."

The shocked expression in his dark eyes made her wish she could retract her words. Clearly, the feeling wasn't mutual.

"Leah—"

She put her fingers to his lips. "Don't. I'm not asking for your love in return. I know I was only a job to you. But you gave me a second chance at life and for that I'll always be grateful."

Releasing her hold on him, she stepped back and wrapped her arms around her middle. "I'd like to meet Sarah now."

Roman stood in Clint Herald's living room, watching the reunion between Leah and Sarah with tears misting his eyes. Tenderness welled in his soul to see the blissful way Leah gazed at the little blond girl with the pretty almond-shaped green eyes of the Renaults. Even though Leah couldn't remember her child, love was evident in the softness of her gaze and the smile on her beautiful face. Roman's insides clenched. She'd gazed at him like that when she confessed her love.

He still couldn't believe she loved him.

But more important, he didn't know how he felt. He couldn't let himself examine his feelings. Not when he wasn't free of his debt to his mother. He had to extract justice for what she'd suffered before he could even think of returning Leah's love.

Clint, standing beside Roman, wiped at his own eyes. "I don't know how we can thank you for bringing Leah back to us."

Uncomfortable with all the mushiness, Roman clapped him on the back. "No thanks needed. I was just doing a job."

Clint gave Roman a funny look. "Right. Well, whatever the case. We're grateful."

Roman nodded in acknowledgment. He'd done what he'd set out to do. Bring down Earl Farley's murderer. Only the murderer had come as a complete shock. Not Leah Farley, as Roman had first assumed, but Charla Renault.

The town was abuzz with the news of Mrs. Renault's break with reality and her killing spree. She would be spending the better portion of her days in a mental institute, while Bosworth would recover from his gunshot wound in the state penitentiary for being Charla Renault's accomplice.

Now it was time for Roman to resume his quest for the man who'd raped his mother and sent her into a suicidal depression.

"Look, tell Leah goodbye for me, will ya?" Roman said as he headed toward the door.

"You should tell her yourself," Clint said with a frown.

Roman gave a negative wave of his hand. "I don't want to interrupt."

He made it out the door and to the sidewalk before he heard the door open behind him.

"You're going to leave without saying goodbye?"

He closed his eyes at the hurt in Leah's voice. "It just seemed easiest."

"For you," she scoffed. She stalked toward him. "Where are you going?"

She knew, he could see it in her eyes. "We've had this discussion."

"And haven't you learned anything?" she said, her hands planted on her hips. "You saw what anger and bitterness did to Charla Renault. You want that to happen to you?"

"I'm going to take care of the anger and the bitterness," he said, not seeing the connection at all.

"Your killing that man won't relieve you of anything. Only God can." Her face softened as she pleaded with him. "Don't you see? You have to accept the past and look to the future."

"I can't."

"If you do this, if you seek justice for what happened to your mother by killing this man, you will only exchange anger for guilt. And the bitterness will never end as long as you have unforgiveness in your heart."

He stepped back, shocked by her accusation. "Are you suggesting I forgive this man? Are you nuts?"

"Forgiveness isn't for him. It's for you. It's so you can find peace and love. So you can let God's love fill you. As long as you harbor unforgiveness in your heart, you'll always be empty and wanting."

Exasperated and irritated by her words, he held up his hands. "Whatever. I'm leaving. I'm really glad you've had your happy ending. Now I need to go get my happy ending to what was started twenty years ago."

Not able to stand the disappointment and pain crumbling in her expression because it hurt too much to know he was the cause, he turned away and strode to where Mort waited in the truck.

No way, no how was he going to forgive his mother's rapist. And he was angry at Leah for throwing that up in his face. She didn't understand his need to make right what he hadn't been able to do as a child.

He had to make sure justice was served. Even if that meant killing a man.

ELEVEN

Leah sank to the ground as Roman climbed into the truck and drove away, out of her life for good.

She hurt so badly for the pain he suffered, but more for the wounds he was about to inflict on his soul.

"Dear Father God, please. Please, don't let him do this. Make him see how wrong he is."

She buried her face in her hands and sobbed for Roman and for herself, for the love crowding her heart for a man who didn't love her back.

"Mommy?"

Sarah's little voice, so scared and uncertain, pulled Leah out of her own misery. Though Leah had no memories of Sarah, her heart recognized her the instant they were reunited. She opened her arms to the child standing a few feet away. Sarah rushed into Leah's embrace. Leah buried her tears in Sarah's downy hair.

Please, God, take care of Roman.

Two days later, Roman's plane touched down in Hattiesburg, at Mississippi's Hattiesburg-Laurel Regional Airport at ten in the morning. He rented a car and bought a map. Plotting out his course for the address provided by his Baton Rouge police buddy, Karl, he resolutely drove down the four-lane highway through the rolling, piney countryside toward the junction that would take him near Lake Serene where, according to the map, Ethan Stumps lived.

At the junction he exited and followed the signs for the lake. About thirteen miles later, he slowed the rented sedan as the street he was searching for appeared on his right. Heart beating like a million birds taking flight, Roman headed down the lane through an older neighborhood full of single-level homes, some of which were badly in need of repair. He slowed as he checked the addresses until finally he stopped in front of a weathered square-shaped house. He got out of the car. Yellowing grass edged the walkway leading to the front door.

Roman fisted his hand and knocked.

From somewhere inside, a television blared. Roman banged harder, fire filling his chest. A moment later, the door opened, revealing a thin, mousey brown-haired woman. Her doelike gaze searched Roman's face. "Yes?"

Roman hesitated. He hadn't done his research. He always did his research, but he'd been so focused on getting to Mississippi and to Stumps that he hadn't checked to see if the scumbag had a family. "Ethan Stumps?"

The woman stepped farther out of the door and pulled it closed behind her. "He's sleeping."

Irritated, Roman said, "Wake him up."

She bit her lip. "Y'all the police?"

Caught off guard by the hope in her eyes, he

blinked. For a moment he thought about lying. But what was the point? "No, ma'am."

Her shoulders sagged and panic entered her eyes. "I won't wake him."

Clearly the woman was afraid of Stumps. "Are you his wife?"

Her lips thinned. "Yeah."

Roman's instincts flared red hot. Stumps was a rapist. It wasn't outside the course of plausibility that he was an abuser, as well. "Are there kids in the house?"

"My Angie's over at the Becks' house," she answered.

"Good. That's good." Roman stepped toward the door. "You might want to go there, as well."

Her eyes rounded before she scurried down the porch stairs and headed toward the street. Roman didn't watch to see where she went. He opened the door of the small house and stepped inside. Though the television boomed from the corner, the living room was empty.

Roman walked down the hall, quietly opening the doors, searching for Stumps. He found the man in the last bedroom, lying facedown and sideways across the bed. The room reeked of cigarettes and booze. A bottle of whiskey lay empty on the floor.

Disgust rose to choke Roman. He kicked the bed.

"Hey!" Stumps grumbled. "Knock it off."

Roman kicked the bed again.

Stumps rolled over, his hand raised as if to strike out at the one who had disturbed his stupor. He froze and his bloodshot eyes widened. "Who are you?"

That face.

For a moment Roman was transported back to that awful night. *The man hitting his mother and forcing her down. Roman rushing in to defend her. The man baring his teeth as his fist slammed into Roman's head, sending him crashing to the floor where he lay bleeding and helpless, watching the man brutalize his mother.*

Roman's rapid breathing echoed inside his head, washing away the terror and bringing in the rage. He stalked forward to yank Stumps off the bed by the leg. Holding him upside down, Roman ground out, "I'm your worst nightmare."

Stump lashed out. Roman easily dodged the ineffective blows as he dropped Stumps onto the floor. "Get up!" Roman yelled.

Stumps scrambled away. "Hey, man, I don't know you. What beef do y'all have with me?"

Roman loomed over the cowering man. "You don't remember me?"

Stumps shook his head. "Should I?"

"Remember Loomis, Louisiana? Remember the Blue Oyster Bar?"

Stumps's muddled gaze showed confusion as he peered up at Roman. "You're that kid."

"That's right." Roman could feel all the hate and rage and bitterness welling up inside until he thought he'd explode. He reached down and grabbed Stumps by the throat, lifting him off the floor.

Fear shone bright in Stumps's hazel eyes. "Hey, man, I'm sorry. I...I got drunk. I can't control myself when I drink. You gotta believe me. Ask Viola." His wild eyed gaze moved toward the door. "Viola!"

"She's not here," Roman snapped. His hand tightened, his fingers digging into Stumps's flesh.

Stumps clawed at Roman's hands. His eyes bulged.

The need to avenge his mother burned hotly in Roman's whole body, searing his soul and his mind.

You'll lose your soul if you make that choice.

Leah's voice resounded in his head. He winced and tried to block her out.

Killing this man will only exchange anger for guilt.

He'd accept the guilt if it meant justice.

As long as you harbor unforgiveness in your heart, you'll always be empty and wanting.

With a guttural growl of unspent rage, Roman released his hold on Stumps's throat and staggered back. Everything inside of him wanted to make this man suffer just as Roman and his mother had suffered. He wanted to kill the man with his bare hands.

But Heaven help him, he couldn't.

He didn't want to be empty and wanting anymore. He wanted to know God's peace. He wanted Leah's love.

He could only accept the past and look to the future. A future he prayed included Leah.

Yanking his cell phone out, Roman dialed 911.

Maybe he couldn't kill the scum, but he could make sure he went to prison for a very long time. There was no statute of limitations on rape in the state of Louisiana.

Overwhelmed, Leah forced a smile as the people gathered in the backyard of the Renaults' home expressed their love and support for her. She couldn't believe that Ava had arranged a homecoming party for her. And here, of all places. But Ava was adamant. Her family had caused this pain; she wanted to start fresh and give her niece's mother a party.

So now Leah was surrounded by a sea of friendly faces that she didn't remember. After about the sixth person she was reintroduced to, she let go of feeling bad and just enjoyed knowing she had so many people in her life who cared.

Shelby sidled up next to her. "I'm so glad you're back."

Leah grinned at the redhead beside her. "Me, too. And thank you for helping Clint so much while I was gone."

Shelby's gaze grew serious. "I love you like a sister, Leah. I'd do anything for you."

Touched, Leah embraced the other woman.

"Hey, you two," Patrick Rivers said as he joined them. "No mushy tears, okay? This is a celebration."

Leah broke away from Shelby with a laugh. She looked forward to getting to know her friend again.

Shelby slid her arm through Patrick's. "Ah, sugar, you know I love you."

Patrick grinned, his eyes alight with love as he gazed at his fiancée. "I love when you call me sugar."

Bittersweet happiness infused Leah. She really was glad her friend had found love. As had Clint with Mandy, the woman he'd hired to nanny Sarah. Leah's gaze sought out her brother. He and Mandy sat on a bench beneath the shade of a cypress.

"Hey, you two, you're monopolizing the guest of

honor," Jocelyn teased as she and her husband, FBI agent Sam Pierce, joined the circle.

Leah accepted Jocelyn's hug with gratitude. "I'm glad you two were able to come. Ava thought you might not."

"Well, Sam and I are working on a case right now, but—" Jocelyn threw Sam a meaningful glance. "Sam has some information we thought you might want to know."

Apprehension and dread trembled through Leah. Was Sam going to tell her Roman had been arrested for murdering the man who'd attacked his mother? Her gaze quickly sought out her daughter, making sure Sarah and Colleen were still in the far corner of the garden watching the koi in the little pond. Once assured Sarah wouldn't overhear anything, Leah braced herself for the heartbreaking news.

"We've been interviewing both Charla and Bosworth extensively and now have a pretty clear picture of the chain of events," Sam said, his intelligent eyes grim.

Leah almost sagged with relief. This wasn't about Roman.

"Wait a sec," Shelby said. "Ava!" She waved over their host. "She'll want to hear this."

Ava and Max moved to stand beside Shelby and Patrick. Others, aware that something was happening, hurried over. Clint and Mandy squeezed in next to Leah. Shelby's cousin, Wendy, apparently another of Leah's friends, jostled her way into the group.

An engaged couple, Jodie Gilmore and FBI Agent Harrison Cahill, whom Leah had been introduced to but no one had said whether she'd known them prior to her amnesia, finished the circle. It seemed everyone had someone. She glanced at Wendy. Well, not everyone. Though Shelby had mentioned that Wendy had been seen with Deputy Olsen of late.

"According to Bosworth, Charla had a very unhappy and abusive childhood," Sam said.

Just as Leah had suspected.

"Oh, no," Ava stated. "I knew she detested my grandfather but I had no idea she'd been… I mean, not that I would." A tear slipped down her pale check. "Mother never spoke of her childhood. For that matter, she barely spoke of anything of a personal nature."

"Maybe you don't want to hear the rest," Max suggested softly.

"No, I need to know. I need to understand," Ava said. To Sam, she said, "Bosworth has been with the Renault family since his boyhood. His father was grandfather's valet. So I'm sure what Bosworth has said is true."

Sam nodded. "Bosworth has tried to protect your mother for years." Sam glanced at Jocelyn. She nodded for him to proceed. "It appears that Bosworth has been in love with your mother since they were children."

"That makes sense. He's always been so attentive to Mother, especially after the car accident," Ava remarked.

"Is the car accident when she supposedly became paralyzed?" Leah asked, feeling a bit awkward for talking so disparagingly about Ava's mother.

Ava sighed. "Yes. The accident killed my father, as well."

Leah's heart went out to the other woman. "I'm so sorry."

"Tell us what you've learned from Charla," Wendy interjected, her voice sounding eager for gossip.

Leah frowned, wondering at this woman whom she'd supposedly been friends with.

"Wendy, please." Shelby hushed her cousin.

"After a psychiatric evaluation, it's been determined that Charla suffers from DID," Jocelyn said. "Dissociative Identity Disorder."

"In other words, she's Sybil," Patrick said.

Jocelyn nodded. "Like the character Sybil. Only in the movie, Sybil had multiple personalities. Charla has only one. With DID, the person may or may not be aware of the other personality. In Charla's saner moments, she does know that something happens to her, but the periods when she is controlled by this other personality are murky and surreal."

"So she's certifiable?" Max asked. "I mean, she won't go to prison but to a mental hospital?"

"Correct," Sam answered.

"And you think that her childhood caused this DID?" Ava asked.

"I do," Jocelyn answered. "In Charla's case, when she felt threatened, a hostile, protective personality would emerge. This personality may have been around for many years before she turned deadly."

"So she really killed Earl, Angelina and her own son, Dylan?" Leah asked. The scope of Charla's madness astounded her.

"She did. Earl apparently threatened to expose Sarah as Dylan's child," Sam said.

Leah winced. The whole world would know now

that she'd been raped by Dylan. But in the grand scheme of things, it was a minor blip. She and her daughter had been reunited. That was all that mattered.

But deep inside, an intense longing for someone to love and be loved by throbbed in Leah. That someone being Roman.

"Do you think Charla was the one who sent me the threatening messages?" Shelby asked with a note of hope in her voice.

This was the first Leah had heard of any threatening notes. She touched Shelby's arm. "What happened?"

"I found a note on the windshield of my car, warning me to keep my mouth shut. I threw it away because I thought it was a prank. Then I opened the book bin like I always do and a snake jumped out at me. Thankfully, Patrick was there to save me."

Leah shivered. "That could have been horrible. Was the snake caught?"

Shelby nodded. "Yep."

"Bosworth confessed to putting the snake in the book bin at the library," Harrison Cahill answered, his oh-so-charming features grim.

"And we compared the pictures of the writing found on the library's mirror to Charla's," Jodie said.

"Another threat?" Leah asked.

"Written in lipstick, no less," Shelby said.

"And?" Patrick said with impatience.

"They don't match Charla," Jodie said. Petite and pretty, the woman held up her hand as Shelby groaned. "We also found your missing Bible in the Renault

Library. The threatening note in the Bible doesn't match Charla's handwriting, either."

"Both of the threatening notes matched Bosworth's handwriting," Harrison said.

Shelby shuddered. "Well, I'm glad they only tried to scare me."

"Hey, that snake could have proved deadly," Patrick said with a scowl.

"Apparently, when you started snooping around, asking questions about Leah, Bosworth thought he could head Charla's destructive side off by trying to scare you," Jodie explained.

"What about Angelina?" Clint asked. "I thought y'all had pretty much decided that Dylan had killed her."

Sam spoke. "Charla found out that Angelina had overheard Earl threaten Dylan. Angelina saw that as an opportunity to blackmail Dylan into marrying her. Charla, with Bosworth's help, killed Angelina and framed Dylan."

"And then Mother killed Dylan?" Ava said, her voice raw. "Why?"

Sam's gaze pierced Leah. "He wanted to sue you for custody of Sarah. Charla wasn't going to let anyone or anything hurt the Renault name. She didn't mean to kill Dylan, though. Evidently, the gun went off accidentally."

"She saw Leah and Sarah as threats, which explains why she hit Leah over the head and dumped her body out in the boonies," Clint said, shaking his head and reaching out for Leah's hand. "I'm sure glad she didn't use her gun that time."

"Me, too." A deep familiar voice from behind Leah echoed the sentiment.

Leah spun around and found herself staring into the dark, brooding gaze of Roman Black. Butterflies took flight in her stomach. Her pulse sang a happy tune. She tried not to let herself get too hopeful. His presence could mean a multitude of things. The best of which could be he'd come back to tell her he loved her. "You're here."

His mouth curved into a smile. "I am."

"I'm glad to see you." She stepped closer and lowered her voice. "Are you... I mean, did everything work out?"

His eyes revealed that he knew exactly what she referred to. He took her hands in his, completely unabashed that they had an audience. "Yes, he's in jail. And now I'm free of that."

She blinked, barely daring to let her thoughts run rampant with possibilities. "Free?"

The dark of his eyes seemed to light up from within. "Free."

She could see the peace in his expression, and her heart soared with thanksgiving. He hadn't killed the man. He'd allowed legal justice to be served for now and to allow God's peace into his life. "I can't tell you how happy that makes me."

"I hope I can make you even happier," he stated, his voice low and husky.

Her mouth went dry. "You do?"

He pulled her closer. "I love you, Leah Farley. You helped me to draw closer to God and to rely on Him for my peace. I want to spend the rest of my life making you happy."

They were surrounded by gasps and giggles and deep chuckles. But Leah didn't care. All she could focus on was the man standing in front of her, declaring his love. Tears of joy crested her lashes. "I love you, too, Roman."

"That's all that matters in life. Your love and God's presence," he stated, and captured her lips. "Now introduce me to the young lady who will be my daughter."

The sound of applause filled the air and cocooned them in a blanket of love. Leah sent up a silent praise to God for a second chance at life. And love with Roman.

* * * * *

Dear Reader,

I hope you enjoyed learning about Leah and Roman as they searched for her identity and the truth of all the murder, mystery and mayhem in Loomis, Louisiana. I found Leah and Roman challenging characters to explore, having so much angst and heartache in their pasts. Roman's need for revenge was a strong, driving force in his life, but it left him empty inside. Only through God's peace and Leah's love was he able to come to terms with the past. For Leah, hiding the past was what set off the awful events of this series. When evil is allowed to live in darkness, it thrives, but when evil is exposed to the light, its power diminishes. A lesson we all must remember.

It's amazing how much of what we go through in life shapes who we become, whether we mean for it to or not. But I know in my heart that every experience, every heartache and triumph has brought me closer to God because I choose to look to God in all circumstances. For through Christ who strengthens me, I can do all things.

May God bless you always,

Terri Reed

QUESTIONS FOR DISCUSSION

1. What made you pick up this book to read? Did it live up to your expectations?

2. Did you think Leah and Roman were realistic characters? Did their romance build believably?

3. Talk about the secondary characters. What did you like or dislike about the people in the story?

4. Was the setting clear and appealing? Could you "see" where the story took place?

5. For Leah, to have no memory of her past must have been frightening. Have you had an experience in the past that was frightening? How did you deal with that fear?

6. Roman burned with the need for revenge. Have you ever wanted to take revenge on someone for something they did? Did you? If so, did you feel better, or worse?

7. Have you read the first five books in this series? If so, talk about the ways the books were connected.

8. Did the suspense element of the story keep you guessing? Why or why not?

9. Did you notice the scripture in the beginning of the book? What application does it have to your life?

10. Did the author's use of language and her writing style make this an enjoyable read? Would you read more from the author?

11. What will be your most vivid memories of this book?

12. What lessons about life, love and faith did you learn from this story?

When a tornado strikes a small Kansas town, Maya Logan sees a new, tender side of her serious boss. Could a family man be lurking beneath Greg Garrison's gruff exterior?

Turn the page for a sneak preview
of their story in
HEALING THE BOSS'S HEART
by Valerie Hansen,
Book 1 in the new six-book
AFTER THE STORM miniseries
available beginning July 2009
from Love Inspired®.

Maya Logan had been watching the skies with growing concern and already had her car keys in hand when she jerked open the door to the office to admit her boss. He held a young boy in his arms. "Get inside. Quick!"

Gregory Garrison thrust the squirming child at her. "Here. Take him. I'm going back after his dog. He refused to come in out of the storm without Charlie."

"Don't be ridiculous." She clutched his arm and pointed. "You'll never catch him. Look." Tommy's dog had taken off running the minute the hail had started.

Debris was swirling through the air in ever-increasing amounts and the hail had begun to pile in lumpy drifts along the curb. It had flattened the flowers she'd so lovingly placed in the planters and buried their stubbly remnants under inches of white, icy crystals.

In the distance, the dog had its tail between its legs and was disappearing into the maelstrom. Unless the frightened animal responded to commands to return, there was no chance of anyone catching up to it.

Gregory took a deep breath and hollered, "Char-lie,"

but Maya could tell he was wasting his breath. The soggy mongrel didn't even slow.

"Take the boy and head for the basement," Gregory yelled at her. Ducking inside, he had to put his shoulder to the heavy door and use his full weight to close and latch it.

She shoved Tommy back at him. "No. I have to go get Layla."

"In this weather? Don't be an idiot."

"She's my daughter. She's only three. She'll be scared to death if I'm not there."

"She's in the preschool at the church, right? They'll take care of the kids."

"No. I'm going after her."

"Use your head. You can't help Layla if you get yourself killed." He grasped her wrist, holding tight.

Maya struggled, twisting her arm till it hurt. "Let me go. I'm going to my baby. She's all I've got."

"That's crazy! A tornado is coming. If the hail doesn't knock you out cold, the tornado's likely to bury you."

"I don't care."

"Yes, you do."

"No, I don't! Let go of me." To her amazement, he held fast. No one, especially a man, was going to treat her this way and get away with it. No one.

"Stop. Think," he shouted, staring at her as if she were deranged.

She continued to struggle, to refuse to give in to his will, his greater strength. "No. *You* think. I'm going to my little girl. That's all there is to it."

"How? Driving?" He indicated the street, which

now looked distorted due to the vibrations of the front window. "It's too late. Look at those cars. Your head isn't half as hard as that metal is and it's already full of dents."

"But…"

She knew in her mind that he was right, yet her heart kept insisting she must do something. Anything. *Please, God, help me. Tell me what to do!*

Her heart was still pounding, her breath shallow and rapid, yet part of her seemed to suddenly accept that her boss was right. That couldn't be. She belonged with Layla. She was her mother.

"We're going to take shelter," Gregory ordered, giving her arm a tug. "Now."

That strong command was enough to renew Maya's resolve and wipe away the calm assurances she had so briefly embraced. She didn't go easily or quietly. Screeching, "No, no, no," she dragged her feet, stumbling along as he pulled and half dragged her toward the basement access.

Staring into the storm moments ago, she had felt as if the fury of the weather was sucking her into a bottomless black hole. Her emotions were still trapped in those murky, imaginary depths, still floundering, sinking, spinning out of control. She pictured Layla, with her silky, long dark hair and beautiful brown eyes.

"If anything happens to my daughter, I'll never forgive you!" she screamed at him.

"I'll take my chances."

Maya knew without a doubt that she'd meant exactly what she'd said. If her precious little girl was hurt, she'd never forgive herself for not trying to reach her. To protect her. And she'd never forgive Gregory Garrison for preventing her from making the attempt. *Never.*

She had to blink to adjust to the dimness of the basement as he shoved her in front of him and forced her down the wooden stairs.

She gasped, coughed. The place smelled musty and sour, totally in character with the advanced age of the building. How long could that bank of brick and stone stores and offices stand against a storm like this? If these walls ever started to topple, nothing would stop their total collapse. Then it wouldn't matter whether they were outside or down here. They'd be just as dead.

That realization sapped her strength and left her almost without sensation. When her boss let go of her wrist and slipped his arm around her shoulders to guide her into a corner next to an abandoned elevator shaft, she was too emotionally numb to continue to fight him. All she could do was pray and continue to repeat, "Layla, Layla," over and over again.

"We'll wait it out here," he said. "This has to be the strongest part of the building."

Maya didn't believe a word he said.

Tommy's quiet sobbing, coupled with her soul-deep concern for her little girl, brought tears to her eyes. She blinked them back, hoping she could control her emotions enough to fool the boy into believing they were all going to come through the tornado unhurt.

As for her, she wasn't sure. Not even the tiniest bit. All she could think about was her daughter. *Dear Lord,* are You watching out for Layla? Please, please, please! Take care of my precious little girl.

* * * * *

See the rest of Maya and Greg's story when
HEALING THE BOSS'S HEART
hits the shelves in July 2009.
And be sure to look for all six of the books
in the AFTER THE STORM series,
where you can follow the residents of
High Plains, Kansas, as they rebuild their
town—and find love in the process.

Copyright © 2009 by Valerie Whisenand

Love**Inspired**®

Maya Logan has always thought of her boss, Greg Garrison, as a hard-nosed type of guy. But when a tornado strikes their small Kansas town, Greg is quick to help however he can, including rebuilding her home. Maya soon discovers that he's building a home for them to share.

Look for

Healing the Boss's Heart

by

Valerie Hansen

Available July
wherever books are sold.

www.SteepleHill.com

Steeple
Hill®

LI87536

REQUEST YOUR FREE BOOKS!

2 FREE RIVETING INSPIRATIONAL NOVELS
PLUS 2 FREE MYSTERY GIFTS

YES! Please send me 2 FREE Love Inspired® Suspense novels and my 2 FREE mystery gifts (gifts are worth about $10). After receiving them, if I don't wish to receive any more books, I can return the shipping statement marked "cancel". If I don't cancel, I will receive 4 brand-new novels every month and be billed just $4.24 per book in the U.S. or $4.74 per book in Canada. That's a savings of over 20% off the cover price. It's quite a bargain! Shipping and handling is just 50¢ per book.* I understand that accepting the 2 free books and gifts places me under no obligation to buy anything. I can always return a shipment and cancel at any time. Even if I never buy another book, the two free books and gifts are mine to keep forever.

123 IDN EYM2 323 IDN EYNE

Name _____ (PLEASE PRINT) _____

Address _____ Apt. # _____

City _____ State/Prov. _____ Zip/Postal Code _____

Signature (if under 18, a parent or guardian must sign) _____

Mail to Steeple Hill Reader Service:
IN U.S.A.: P.O. Box 1867, Buffalo, NY 14240-1867
IN CANADA: P.O. Box 609, Fort Erie, Ontario L2A 5X3

Not valid to current subscribers of Love Inspired Suspense books.

Want to try two free books from another series?
Call 1-800-873-8635 or visit www.morefreebooks.com

* Terms and prices subject to change without notice. Prices do not include applicable taxes. Sales tax applicable in N.Y. Canadian residents will be charged applicable provincial taxes and GST. Offer not valid in Quebec. This offer is limited to one order per household. All orders subject to approval. Credit or debit balances in a customer's account(s) may be offset by any other outstanding balance owed by or to the customer. Please allow 4 to 6 weeks for delivery. Offer available while quantities last.

Your Privacy: Steeple Hill Books is committed to protecting your privacy. Our Privacy Policy is available online at www.SteepleHill.com or upon request from the Reader Service. From time to time we make our lists of customers available to reputable third parties who may have a product or service of interest to you. If you would prefer we not share your name and address, please check here. ☐

Love Inspired

TITLES AVAILABLE NEXT MONTH

Available June 30, 2009

SECOND CHANCE FAMILY by Margaret Daley
Fostered by Love

Whitney Maxwell is about to get a lesson in trust—and family—from an unexpected source: her student Jason. As she and his single dad, Dr. Shane McCoy, try to help Jason deal with his autism, she realizes her dream of a forever family is right in front of her.

HEALING THE BOSS'S HEART by Valerie Hansen
After the Storm

When a tornado strikes her small Kansas town, single mom Maya Logan sees an unexpected side of her boss. Greg Garrison's tender care for her family and an orphaned boy make her wonder if he's hiding a family man beneath his gruff exterior.

LONE STAR CINDERELLA by Debra Clopton

The town matchmakers have cowboy Seth Turner in mind for history teacher Melody Chandler, but all he seems to want to do is stop her from researching his family history. Seth's afraid of what she'll find, especially when he realizes it's a place in his heart.

BLUEGRASS BLESSINGS by Allie Pleiter
Kentucky Corners

Cameron Rollings may be a jaded city boy, but God led him to Kentucky for a reason, and baker Dinah Hopkins plans to help him count his bluegrass blessings.

HOMETOWN COURTSHIP by Diann Hunt

Brad Sharp fully expects his latest community service volunteer, Callie Easton, to slack off on their Make-a-Home project. But her golden heart and willingness to work makes Brad take a second look, one that could last forever.

RETURN TO LOVE by Betsy St. Amant

Penguin keeper Gracie Broussard needs to find a new home for her beloved birds. If only Carter Alexander, the man who broke her heart years ago, wasn't the only one who could help. Carter promises that he's changed, and he's determined to show Gracie that love is a place you can always return to.

LICNMBPA0609